Steck-Vaughn

BRIDGES TO READING COMPREHENSION

Level B

Steck-Vaughn
COMPANY
ELEMENTARY • SECONDARY • ADULT • LIBRARY

ACKNOWLEDGMENTS

EXECUTIVE EDITOR: Diane Sharpe

PROJECT EDITOR: Anne Souby

DESIGN MANAGER: Donna Brawley

ELECTRONIC PRODUCTION (COVER): Alan Klemp

PHOTO EDITOR: Margie Foster

PRODUCT DEVELOPMENT: Curriculum Concepts

ILLUSTRATION CREDITS: Cover Adolph Gonzalez; Unit 1 Charles Shaw: p.24-28, 30-32; Unit 2 Gershom Griffith: p.54-59, 61-62; Judy Love: p.64-69, 71-72; Unit 3 Loretta Lustig: p.116-121, 123-125.

PHOTO CREDITS: Unit 1 p.4 © Carl Frank/Photo Researchers; p.6 © Stephanie Myers; p.7 © Porterfield Chickering/Photo Researchers; p.8 © Margaret McCarthy/Peter Arnold, Inc.; p.9 © David Young-Wolff/PhotoEdit; p.10 © Stephanie Myers; p.11 (a-g, i-l) © Cooke Photographics, (h) © Bill Records; p.12 © Porterfield Chickering/Photo Researchers; p.13 © Margaret McCarthy/Peter Arnold, Inc.; p.14 © Stephen Ogilvy; p.15 © Louise Gubb/JB Pictures; pp.16-17 © Wide World Photos; p.18 © Louise Gubb/JB Pictures; p.19 © Wide World Photos; p. 20 © Cooke Photographics; p.21 © Louise Gubb/JB Pictures; p.23 © Wide World Photos; p.29 (a-b, d-h, k-l) © Cooke Photographics, (i) © David Omer, (j) © Zig Leszczynski/Animals Animals; p.33 © Wide World Photos; p.34 © Movie Still Archives; p.35 © UPI/Bettmann; p.36 © Mark Burnet/PhotoEdit; p.37 © Wide World Photos; p.38 (a) © TX Highways, (b) © Patti Murray/Animals Animals, (c-f, h-j) © Cooke Photographics, (g) © David Omer; p.39 © Mark Burnet/PhotoEdit; p.40 © Movie Still Archives; p.41 © UPI/Bettmann; Unit 2 p.42 (spider web) © Fotopic/Omni-Photo Communications, (Easter Island) © George Holton/Photo Researchers; pp.44-45 © Tom McHugh/Photo Researchers; p.46 © Photo Researchers; p.47 © UPI/Bettmann; p.48 © NYZS/The Wildlife Conservation Society; p.49 © Tom McHugh/Photo Researchers; p.50 (a) © Tom McHugh/Photo Researchers, (b) © Breck Kent, (c-f) © Cooke Photographics, (g) © Joe McDonald/Animals Animals, (h) © Bill Records; p.51 © UPI/Bettmann; p.53 © NYZS/The Wildlife Conservation Society; p.60 (a, h) © Cooke Photographics, (b-e) © David Omer, (f) © Stephen Dalton/Animals Animals, (g) © Patti Murray/Animals Animals; p.70 © David Omer; pp.74-79 © The Jane Goodall Institute; p.80 (a, c-d) © David Omer, (b) © Cooke Photographics; pp.81-83 © The Jane Goodall Institute; Unit 3 p.84 (monkey) © 1994 Busch Entertainment Corporation. All rights reserved; (King Kong) © 1933 RKO Pictures, Inc. All rights reserved; p.86 © 1994 Busch Entertainment Corporation. All rights reserved; p.87 © Tom McHugh/NAS/Photo Researchers; p.88 © Paul A. Zahl, PhD/National Geographic Society; p.89 © Robert C. Hermes/NAS/Photo Researchers; p.90 © NYZS/The Wildlife Conservation Society; p.91 © Tom McHugh/NAS/Photo Researchers; p.92 (a) © Stephen Dalton/Animals Animals, (b-c) © Cooke Photographics, (d) © Arnie Katz/Unicorn; p.93 © Robert C. Hermes/NAS/Photo Researchers; p.95 © NYZS/The Wildlife Conservation Society; p.96 © Richard Nowitz/Photo Researchers; p.97 © 1994 Busch Entertainment Corporation. All rights reserved; p.98 © Hamleys; p.99 © Rahn & Associates; p.100 © North Hills News Record; p.101 © Richard Nowitz/Photo Researchers; p.102 (a, c) © Grant Heilman, (b, d) © Cooke Photographics; p.103 © Hamleys; p.104 © 1994 Busch Entertainment Corporation. All rights reserved; p.105 © North Hills News Record; p.106 Movie Still Archives; p.111 (King Kong) © 1933 RKO Pictures, Inc. All rights reserved; p.112 (a, c) © Cooke Photographics, (b, d) © Jim Wiener/Photo Researchers; p.115 Movie Still Archives; p.122 (b) © Lick Observatory, (d, g-j) © David Omer, (e-f) © Cooke Photographics.

ISBN 0–8114–5742–7

CONTENTS

1 MUSIC FOR EVERYONE

Why do we have music?

Music is for fun. It's also for important times. Music helps us say what we feel. Music helps people tell about ideas. People play music everywhere in the world. You will learn more about music and the people who make it as you read this unit.

What Do You Already Know?

Have you ever sung with other people? Have you played music with your friends? What kind of music do you like? Write about how music makes you feel.

____

____

____

____

____

____

What Do You Want to Find Out?

What would you like to know about music? What would you like to find out about the people who make music? You might learn about these things in this unit. On the lines below, write the questions you would like answered.

____

____

____

____

____

____

GETTING READY TO READ

This unit begins with a story called "Making Music Around the World." Do you know anything about music from other countries? Can you imagine what instruments people use to make music in Africa?

What Do You Think You Will Learn?

Look through "Making Music Around the World" on pages 7 through 9. What do you think you will learn as you read this story? Write your ideas below.

____

____

____

____

____

MAKING MUSIC AROUND THE WORLD

People all over the world play music. They use drums, bells, chimes, and horns. They use many other instruments, too. Music has different sounds in different places.

Music Is Everywhere

Music comes from many places. Do you like the sound of a guitar? The guitar comes from Spain. Have you ever clapped to the beat of gospel music? The gospel beat began in Africa.

Native Americans have their own sound of music. They use drums and rattles. Songs are a very important part of their music.

In the West Indies, people play oil drums. The drum tops have different shapes. Each shape makes a different sound.

Drums and Rattles

Drums and rattles are part of the music of Africa. People who make music begin early. They learn when they are small children. Musicians are thought to be very special.

Music is played on all the important days in people's lives. Musicians play music when babies are born. They make music when young people become adults. They make music when men and women marry. They play music when people die.

Gongs and Chimes

Chinese music today often sounds just like the music of long ago. The Chinese were playing music 3,000 years ago! Music was played for people in palaces. It was also used for putting on plays. Today the music is for everyone. Musicians use gongs and chimes. They play long instruments with strings.

Music has been around for a very long time. It is important in the lives of all people. Think about the next song you hear. See if you can tell where the song comes from.

Gongs are used in the music of Asia.

AFTER READING

What Did You Learn?

You have read "Making Music Around the World" for the first time. Look back at what you wrote on page 6. Did you learn what you thought you would learn? What were you surprised to learn? Write your answers below.

____

____

____

Check Your Understanding

Darken the circle next to the word that best completes each sentence.

1. In Africa, people play music on important ______.

   Ⓐ guitars   Ⓑ days   Ⓒ children

2. Music makers in Africa learn to play ______ when they are children.

   Ⓐ chimes   Ⓑ games   Ⓒ music

3. An important part of Native American music is ______.

   Ⓐ songs   Ⓑ guitars   Ⓒ chimes

4. The guitar comes from ______.

   Ⓐ Spain   Ⓑ China   Ⓒ Africa

5. Chinese music is ______ years old.

   Ⓐ 3,000   Ⓑ 300   Ⓒ 30

Word Analysis — Short a and e

Ham has the **short a** vowel sound.

Jet has the **short e** vowel sound.

Say each picture name. Write a or e if you hear a short vowel sound.

1.

2.

3.

4.

5.

6.

7.

8.

Say each picture name. Circle the story word that has the same short vowel sound.

9. 

play

lands

mat

days

10. 

drums

bells

net

see

Vocabulary — Context Clues

What do you do when you don't know the meaning of a word? You can look at the words around it. Look at these sentences.

People play drums, bells, chimes, and horns. They use many other instruments, too.

You can tell the meaning of instruments from the words around it. Drums and horns make music. An instrument must be a thing that makes music.

Read these sentences. Look at the word in dark print. Underline the words that help you tell its meaning. Write what the word means.

1. People who play music are special. These **musicians** bring joy to all who hear them.

   ____

2. Music is played at **celebrations**. Happy times and music go together.

   ____

3. Some music has a special **melody**. Its tune is easy to remember.

   ____

Words That Were New to You

Choose words from the story that were new to you. Use a dictionary to check the meanings. Add the words and their meanings to your word list on page 126.

REREADING

Main Idea and Details

Most writers have something they want to tell you. This is called the **main idea**. The main idea tells the most important idea in a story. Other pieces of information in the story tell more about the main idea. These are called **details**.

Look at the main idea and some of the details about African music on page 8.

Main Idea: Music is played on all the important days in people's lives.

DETAIL: Musicians play music when babies are born.

DETAIL: They make music when young people become adults.

DETAIL: They make music when men and women marry.

Read each group of three sentences. Write **M** for main idea. Write **D** for details.

1. _____ The guitar comes from Spain.

   _____ The gospel beat began in Africa.

   _____ Music comes from many places.

2. _____ Songs are a very important part of Native American music.

   _____ Native Americans have their own sound of music.

   _____ They use drums and rattles.

THINK and WRITE

Use what you have learned to complete one of these activities.

1. Do you play an instrument? If not, there is probably one special instrument whose sound you really like. Write down the name of your favorite instrument and tell why you like it.

2. Make a poster about music from around the world. Draw and write things to show the different countries and instruments.

3. Make up a song to celebrate a special time. Sing your song to someone.

4. Make your own instruments. You can try using different things to make rattles and drums. When you are done, tell how you made your instruments.

This girl is filling the box with beans to make a rattle. She will use the cans as drums.

GETTING READY TO READ

You are about to read about a famous singing group. The group is from South Africa. It is called Ladysmith Black Mambazo. The leader of the group is Joseph Shabalala. He had a dream about music. What do you think his dream was?

What Do You Think You Will Learn?

Look through "Shabalala and the Black Axe" on pages 16 through 18. What are some things you think you might learn as you read this story? Write your ideas below.

Shabalala and the Black Axe

Joseph Shabalala is from South Africa. He grew up on a farm in the grasslands. The nearest city was Ladysmith. Shabalala thought about music all the time. He liked to think about the sounds on the farm. He heard music in the sounds of the animals. Each sound was different.

The Music in His Thoughts

Shabalala wanted to sing the music that he heard around him. He put together a group. He called the group "Ladysmith Black Mambazo." The name means "the black axe of Ladysmith." An axe is used to cut wood for cooking. It is used to build houses. Shabalala believes music is just as important as food and a place to live.

Shabalala and Ladysmith Black Mambazo sing on a television show.

Angel Voices

In 1985, American superstar Paul Simon went to South Africa. Simon is famous for the songs he writes and sings. He went to South Africa to make a record. He wanted to use sounds and beats from that country. One day he heard Ladysmith Black Mambazo. He loved their sound.

Paul Simon asked Ladysmith Black Mambazo to sing on the record. The record was called *Graceland*. It was a big hit! People all over the world bought *Graceland*.

Paul Simon and Ladysmith Black Mambazo gave many shows for people. They went around the world together. Some people said Shabalala and his singers had voices like angels.

Paul Simon and Ladysmith Black Mambazo made wonderful music together.

Following His Heart

Today, Shabalala teaches at a college in South Africa. He also goes to different villages to help people with their singing. Shabalala believes that music is one way for people to get to know each other. He thinks that it is important to sing. He keeps looking for ways to use the sounds from the farm. That way others will get to know about his people.

And the Beat Goes On

Ladysmith Black Mambazo keeps singing. The group keeps making people happy and sad with music. The music is broadcast all over the world. As Shabalala says, "When you are singing, you are free."

AFTER READING

What Did You Learn?

You have read "Shabalala and the Black Axe" for the first time. Look back at what you wrote on page 15. Did you learn what you thought you would learn? What were you surprised to find out? Write your answers below.

____

____

____

Check Your Understanding

Darken the circle next to the word that best completes each sentence.

1. Joseph Shabalala wanted to _______.

   Ⓐ cook   Ⓑ build houses   Ⓒ sing

2. Shabalala decided to put together a _______ to sing music.

   Ⓐ school   Ⓑ group   Ⓒ meeting

3. Paul Simon went to South Africa to make a _______.

   Ⓐ record   Ⓑ axe   Ⓒ farm

4. Simon and Ladysmith Black Mambazo made a record named _______ together.

   Ⓐ *Graceland*   Ⓑ Grassland   Ⓒ Ladysmith

Word Analysis — Short i, o, and u

Fish has the **short i** vowel sound.

Mop has the **short o** vowel sound.

Rug has the **short u** vowel sound.

Say each picture name. Write **i**, **o**, or **u** if you hear a short vowel sound.

1. 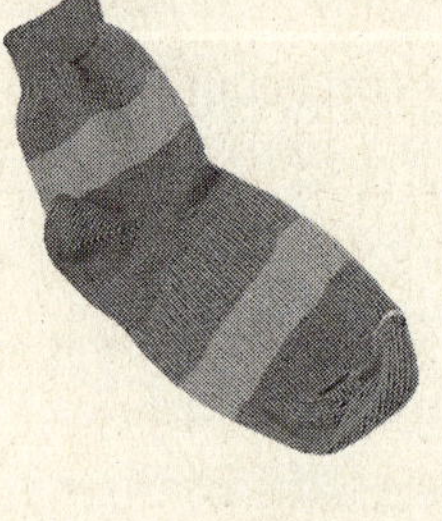

2. 

3. 

4. 

Say the word in dark print. Listen for the short vowel sound. Read the sentence from the story. Circle the word in the sentence that has the same short vowel sound as the word in dark print.

fish   He liked to think about the sounds on the farm.

rug   An axe is used to cut wood for cooking.

mop   Ladysmith Black Mambazo sings on a television show.

Vocabulary — Compound Words

Sometimes a word is made up of two smaller words. The larger word is called a **compound word**. Look at this sentence.

> Joseph Shabalala grew up in the grasslands in South Africa.

Grasslands is made up of two smaller words, grass and lands. Think about what each word means. Grasslands probably means "lands of grass."

Read these sentences. Circle the compound word in each sentence. Write the two smaller words that make up the compound word.

1. Ladysmith Black Mambazo is an outstanding singing group.

   _______________________   _______________________

2. Simon and Shabalala have a great friendship.

   _______________________   _______________________

3. Joseph Shabalala would daydream about music.

   _______________________   _______________________

4. Paul Simon is a superstar.

   _______________________   _______________________

Words That Were New to You

Choose words from the story that were new to you. Use a dictionary to check the meanings. Add the words and their meanings to your word list on page 126.

REREADING

Sequence

Things happen in a story in a certain order. This order is important. It helps you keep track of what is happening in a story.

Look at this chart. It can help you keep track of what happened in the story.

1. What happened first?	Joseph Shabalala lived on a farm.
2. What happened next?	Joseph Shabalala formed Ladysmith Black Mambazo.
3. What happened last?	The music they made is heard around the world.

Reread "Shabalala and the Black Axe." Think about the order in which things happened. Write 1, 2, or 3 in front of each sentence below to show the right order.

______ The record was a big hit.

______ Paul Simon loved Ladysmith Black Mambazo's music.

______ Paul Simon and Ladysmith Black Mambazo made a record.

Main Idea and Details

A **main idea** is the most important idea in a paragraph. The **details** tell more about the main idea. Write two details that tell more about each main idea below. Use the story to help you.

1. Main Idea: Shabalala wanted to sing the music that he heard around him. (page 16)

    DETAIL: _______________________________________

    DETAIL: _______________________________________

2. Main Idea: Paul Simon asked Ladysmith Black Mambazo to sing on the record. (page 17)

    DETAIL: _______________________________________

    DETAIL: _______________________________________

THINK and WRITE

Use what you have learned to complete one of these activities.

1. If you were going to name a singing group, what would you call it? Why? Write your answers.

2. Imagine you are either Paul Simon or Joseph Shabalala. Write in your diary about the day you met. Tell what happened.

3. What song would you like to hear Ladysmith Black Mambazo sing? Tell why.

GETTING READY TO READ

You are about to read "Gary's Guitar." Would you like to play a guitar? Can you imagine what it would be like to play guitar with your friends?

What Do You Think You Will Learn?

Look through "Gary's Guitar" on pages 25 through 27. What do you think this story is about? Write your ideas below.

____

____

____

____

____

____

Gary was shy. When someone talked to him, he couldn't think of anything to say. And what was worse, he turned pink! More and more he stayed away from people. He felt very alone.

One day Gary's mom brought him a present. It was a big shiny guitar. Gary was really happy. First, his mom showed him how to hold it. Then she placed three of the fingers of his left hand on the strings. "Push down hard," she said. "Now take your right thumb and strum the strings."

A neat sound came out. "Wow! Mom, show me more!" he yelled. Mom showed him two more ways to put his left fingers on the strings.

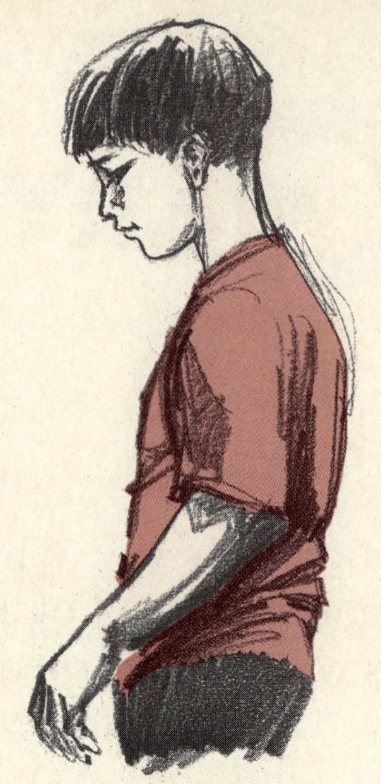

"Each different sound is called a chord," she explained. "Listen to what happens when you play them one after the other."

Mom played one chord. She played another. "You can sing many songs when you can play a few chords," Mom said.

Gary started playing his guitar every day. He learned many songs.

One day a note came in the mail. Gary was invited to Carrie Anderson's birthday party.

"Oh, please, Mom," cried Gary. "I don't want to go. I'll turn pink if anyone talks to me."

"Well, why don't you take your guitar," Mom said. "Think about it."

Gary thought for a while. Maybe he'd be able to talk about the guitar. Or maybe he could play it and not talk at all! "Well . . . okay," he said.

As soon as Gary got to the party, Mike Stone asked, "What are you doing with that?"

"I thought that I might play some songs," said Gary. He strummed a few chords. The hard work had paid off. They sounded pretty good!

"Sing a song," someone asked.

Gary sang his favorite song. Then he sang two more. All the kids listened. Then they clapped and cheered. When he was finished, it was time to eat. As Gary sat down to eat, Angela Gomez asked, "How do you like our new soccer coach?"

"I think she's really cool," said Gary.

"Me, too," said Angela.

Gary talked with all the kids. Before he knew it, the party was over. He was happy. He had played his guitar. He had talked. He hadn't turned pink. He'd had a really good time!

AFTER READING

What Did You Learn?

You've just read "Gary's Guitar" for the first time. Now look back at what you wrote on page 24. Did you make a good guess about what the story was about? What surprised you in the story? Write your answers below.

____

____

____

Check Your Understanding

Darken the circle next to the word that best completes each sentence.

1. Gary had a hard time talking to people because he was very _______.

Ⓐ shy   Ⓑ tall   Ⓒ happy

2. Gary's mom taught him how to play _______.

Ⓐ baseball   Ⓑ drums   Ⓒ guitar

3. Carrie Anderson invited Gary to a _______.

Ⓐ picnic   Ⓑ party   Ⓒ dance

4. After singing, Gary _______ with people.

Ⓐ played   Ⓑ talked   Ⓒ left

5. Gary was happy he did not turn _______.

Ⓐ pink   Ⓑ sad   Ⓒ right

Word Analysis — Long Vowel Sounds
a, e, i, o, u

Say each picture name. Write the letter that stands for each long vowel sound.

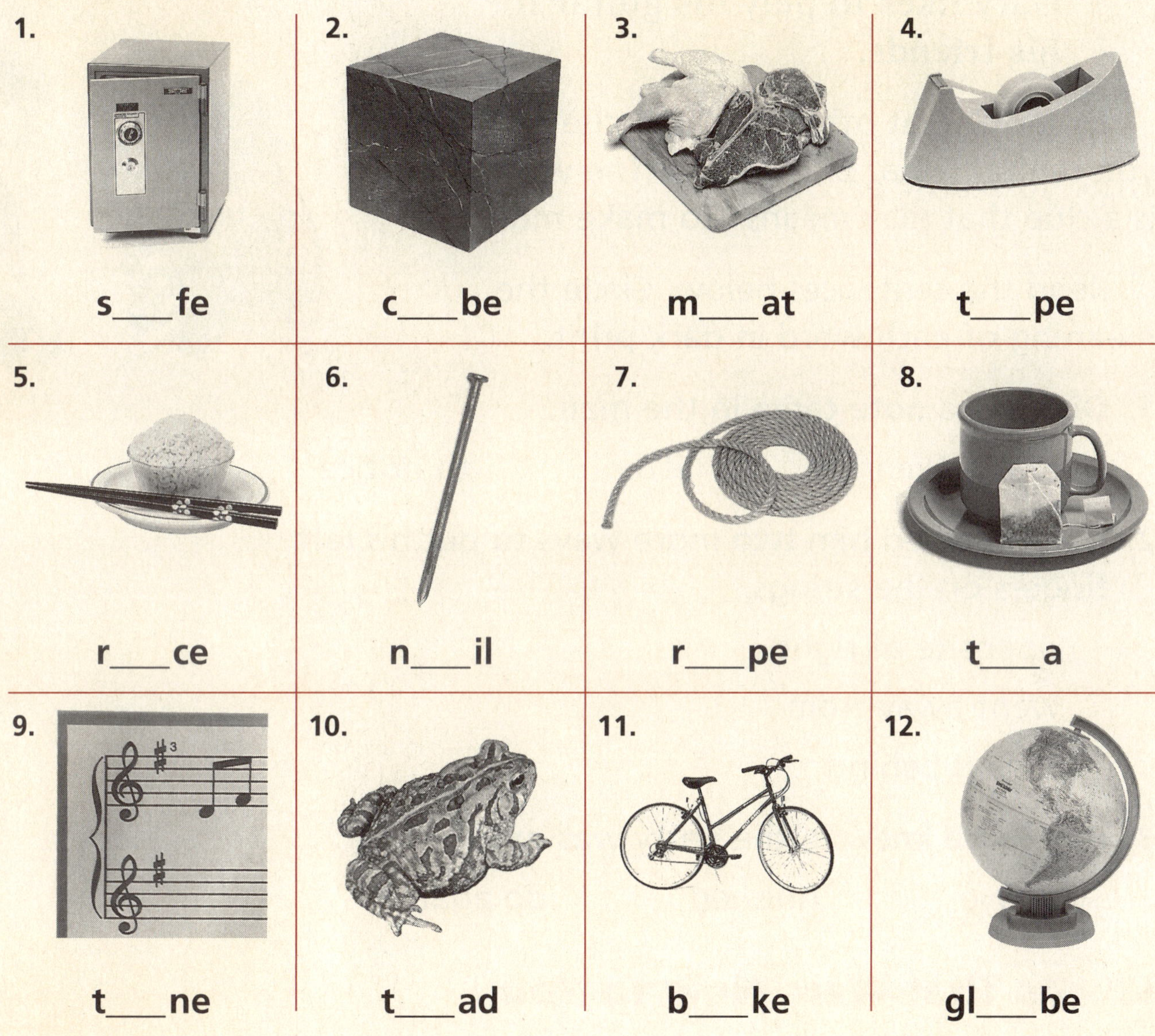

1. s___fe
2. c___be
3. m___at
4. t___pe
5. r___ce
6. n___il
7. r___pe
8. t___a
9. t___ne
10. t___ad
11. b___ke
12. gl___be

Look back at the story. Find two words that have the same vowel sound you hear in **safe**.

Write the words here.

_________________________ _________________________

Vocabulary — Multiple Meanings

Some words have more than one meaning. The word play can mean "to make music" or "a show that is acted on a stage." Read this sentence.

Gary likes to play his guitar for his friends.

By looking at other words in the sentence, you can tell what play means. The word guitar is a clue that play means "to make music."

Read the sentences below. Circle the meaning of each word in dark print.

1. One day a **note** came in the mail.

   musical mark   letter   to notice

2. Mom showed him two more ways to put his **left** fingers on the strings.

   opposite of right

   went away from

   stayed behind

3. Before he knew it, the party was **over**.

   above   finished   do again

Words That Were New to You

Choose words from the story that were new to you. Use a dictionary to check the meanings. Add the words and their meanings to your word list on page 126.

REREADING

Referents

A **noun** is the name of a person, place, or thing. A **pronoun** can take the place of a noun in a sentence. The words below are pronouns.

| I | he | she | they | we | it | you |

Read these sentences.

> One day Gary's mom brought him a present. It was a big shiny guitar.

The word **present** is a noun. The word **it** is a pronoun. **It** stands for **present**.

Read these sentences. The words in dark print are pronouns. Circle the noun that each pronoun stands for.

1. Gary was shy. **He** stayed away from people.

2. Mom played one chord. **She** played another.

3. The children listened. Then **they** clapped and cheered.

Reread "Gary's Guitar." Find one place where a pronoun stands for a noun. Write the sentences on the lines below. Underline the noun. Circle the pronoun.

Sequence

Remember that it's important to know the order that things happen in a story. Read these sentences. Then put them in the right order. Write 1, 2, 3, or 4 on the lines before each sentence.

_______ Gary played his guitar at the party.

_______ Mom showed Gary how to play guitar.

_______ Gary felt alone because he was so shy.

_______ Mom brought Gary a guitar.

THINK and WRITE

Use what you have learned to complete one of these activities.

1. What do you think would have happened at the party if Gary had not brought the guitar? Write what you think would have happened.

2. Imagine that Gary plays his guitar at a school dance. Write about what happens at the dance.

3. Do you feel shy when you meet new people? Write how you feel when you meet someone new.

4. Gary took his guitar to the party to share. What other instruments can people play at parties? Tell about them.

GETTING READY TO READ

You are about to read "Movie Music." Do you have favorite music from a movie? What do you think movies would be like without music?

What Do You Think You Will Learn?

Look through "Movie Music" on pages 34 through 36. What do you think you will learn as you read this story? Write your ideas below.

____

____

____

____

____

Movie Music

Have you ever wondered how the music gets into a movie? You can't see anyone playing. But the music is very much there. How do they do that?

People Working Together

Many people work on a movie before the music is even written. You see only the actors. But there are many other jobs that need to be done to make a movie.

The Director

The most important person is the director. The director tells the actors what to do. She tells everyone else what to do, too. She's at the center of all the action! She works with everyone to make hours and hours of film.

The Editor

After filming, the director works with the editor. They decide which parts of the movie are the best. The director has a general idea of which parts she wants to keep. Then the editor cuts the other parts. This is called editing. The part of the movie that is left is called a rough cut.

Many people look at the rough cut. They give ideas about other changes to make. Then the director and the editor make the changes. This new movie is called the fine cut.

Leonard Bernstein was a famous composer. He wrote the music for "West Side Story."

And Now the Music!

A composer writes the music for a movie. The composer and the director work with the fine cut. They decide where to put music in the movie. The composer writes the music. Then musicians record the music for the movie.

The Mixers

The composer and the director now work with the mixers. Mixers put together the fine cut and the recording of the music. Now the movie has pictures and music. This is the final cut.

The Final Cut

The next time you see a movie, remember that you are seeing the final cut. Listen for the music. Think about the director. Think about the editor. Think about the composer. Would you choose the same music to put in the movie? Do you like where the mixers put the music? Would you add music in other places? What would you do? What kind of movie would you like to make?

AFTER READING

What Did You Learn?

You have read "Movie Music" for the first time. Look back at what you wrote on page 33. Did you learn what you thought you would learn? What surprised you? Write your answers below.

____

____

____

Check Your Understanding

Read each sentence. Look at the words in the box. Choose one to complete each sentence. Write the word on the correct line.

editor	composer	final
mixers	director	

1. The _________________ is in charge of the movie.

2. The _________________ makes the movie shorter.

3. The music is written by the _________________.

4. The _________________ put the music and movie together.

5. People see the _________________ cut of a movie.

Word Analysis — Soft c and g

When **c** comes before **e**, **i**, or **y**, it can have the **soft c** sound that you hear in **city**.

When **g** comes before **e**, **i**, or **y**, it can have the **soft g** sound that you hear in **giraffe**.

Say the name of the first picture in each row. Circle the words that have the same **c** or **g** sound.

1.

| rice | mice | cup | pencil |

2.

| stage | dog | egg | cage |

Look at page 35 of the story. Find two words that have the **soft g** sound. Write the words on the lines below.

_______________________   _______________________

Vocabulary — Inflectional Endings

A **verb** is a word that shows action. A verb tells what a person, place, or thing does. When you add -s or -es to a verb, the action is happening in the present. When you add -ed to a verb, the action happened in the past. Read these sentences.

1. The director looks at the film every day.

2. The director looked at the film last night.

In sentence 1, the action is happening in the present. It tells what the director is doing now. In sentence 2, the action happened in the past. It tells what the director did last night.

Read these sentences. Is the action happening now or did it happen in the past? Circle the word that best completes each sentence.

1. She _______ to many songs yesterday before she chose that one.

   listens   listened

2. The composer _______ with the director now.

   works   worked

3. Everyone _______ a movie last night.

   watches   watched

Words That Were New to You

Choose words from the story that were new to you. Use a dictionary to check the meanings. Add the words and their meanings to your word list on page 126.

REREADING

Drawing Conclusions

Sometimes you have to figure out what a writer means in a story. You can do this by using story clues and your own good sense. That is called **drawing conclusions**. Read these sentences.

> The director works with the actors.
> The director also works with the
> mixers and the editor.

These sentences tell you what the director does. The director works with everyone. You could draw the conclusion that the director is the most important person who works on a movie.

Reread the story. Then darken the circle that tells the conclusion you would draw.

1. Most movies have music. A composer writes music. A director works with a composer.

    Ⓐ Music is an important part of a movie.

    Ⓑ Most directors don't care about the music.

    Ⓒ Movie music is pretty.

2. The director and editor make a rough cut of the movie. Then people look at the rough cut. The director and editor make more changes and make a fine cut.

    Ⓐ The rough cut is easy to make.

    Ⓑ The fine cut is better than the rough cut.

    Ⓒ The editor works hard.

Word Referents

Read these sentences. The word in dark print is a pronoun. Circle the noun it stands for.

1. Steven Spielberg is a director. **He** made *E.T.*

2. *E.T.* was a good movie. **It** was about someone from another planet.

3. Many people loved *E.T.* **They** saw it over and over again.

THINK and WRITE

Use what you have learned to complete one of these activities.

1. Imagine that you are the director of a movie. Write a plan for how to make a movie. Put in all of the steps.

2. What job would you like to have on a movie? Tell why.

3. Suppose you are a composer for a movie. It is a scary mystery movie. Write a note to the director telling the kind of music you want to use. Tell which musicians or singers you would like to play and sing the music.

4. Think about a movie you have seen. Was the movie music loud or soft? Did it have words? Tell about it.

2 MYSTERIES

What is a mystery?

A mystery is a puzzle. Something happened! No one knows how it happened. Most people like a good mystery. They like to try to find out what happened. As you read this unit, you will find out about different kinds of mysteries.

What Do You Already Know?

Think about mysteries you have seen in the movies or on TV. Did you wonder, "Who did it?" Did you think, "How could that happen?" Write about a mystery you've seen.

____

____

____

____

____

____

What Do You Want to Find Out?

What mysteries would you like to find out about? On the lines below, write some questions you would like answered. You may find the answers as you read the unit.

____

____

____

____

____

GETTING READY TO READ

The first story you will read is about a very strange animal. It is called a platypus. Have you ever heard of this animal? What do you think might be strange about it? Why do you think it is a mystery?

What Do You Think You Will Learn?

Look through "What Is a Platypus?" on pages 45 through 48. Look at the pictures. What do you think you will learn in the story? Write your ideas below.

____

____

____

____

What Is a PLATYPUS?

Look at this picture of a platypus. What kind of animal do you think it is? Here are some clues. See if you can solve the mystery!

Clue 1 — The Platypus Lives Near Water

The platypus swims as well as a fish. It lives along streams. It catches its food at the bottom of the streams. The platypus spends most of its life in the water. But it can also move around on land.

The platypus uses its feet to help it swim.

Clue 2 — The Platypus Has a Bill

The platypus has a bill like a duck. But the platypus doesn't quack! It uses its bill like a shovel. The bill helps it dig for food.

Clue 3 — The Platypus Has Webbed Feet

The platypus has feet like a duck. Thin skin grows between the toes on the feet of a platypus. The skin makes a web.

So, the platypus has webbed feet like a duck. It has a bill like a duck. It stays in the water most of the time. Could the platypus be a water bird like a duck?

Clue 4 — The Platypus Lays Eggs

The platypus lays eggs. So does a duck. But a duck's eggs are smooth. Platypus eggs have a thick covering. They feel like shoe leather.

Reptiles like lizards, snakes, and alligators lay eggs that feel like shoe leather. Some reptiles can also live on the land and in the water. Could the platypus be a reptile?

A baby platypus hatches from an egg. It is less than six inches long.

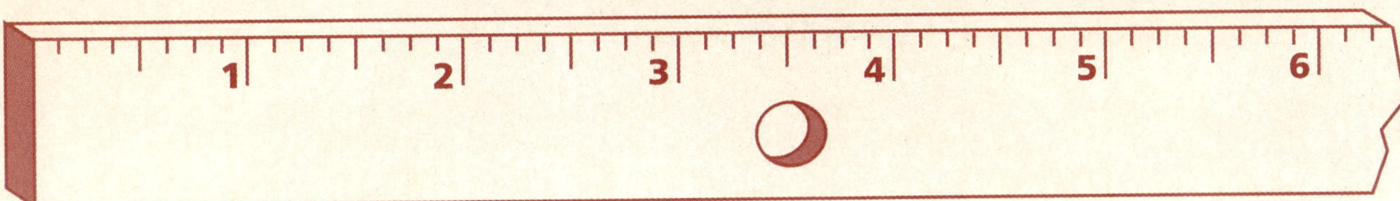

Clue 5 — The Platypus Has Fur

The platypus has thick, dark fur. Reptiles don't have fur! So, the platypus can't be a reptile. What kind of animal could the platypus be?

Clue 6 — Platypus Babies Get Milk from Their Mothers

Some animals get milk from their mothers. These animals are called mammals. Baby animals like puppies, kittens, and baby whales get milk from their mothers. They are mammals.

Some mammals also have fur. The platypus has fur. Platypus babies get milk from their mothers. Could the platypus be a mammal?

The Mystery Is Solved!

The platypus is a mammal! But it's different from almost all other mammals. Most mammals do not lay eggs. The platypus and the spiny anteater are the only ones that do!

Now you know what kind of animal the platypus is. But in some ways, it is still a mystery!

The platypus is one of the strangest animals in the world.

AFTER READING

What Did You Learn?

You have read "What Is a Platypus?" for the first time. What did you think you would learn? Look back at what you wrote on page 44. What did you learn that surprised you? Write your answers below.

____

____

____

Check Your Understanding

Darken the circle next to the word that best completes each sentence.

1. The platypus has a _______ like a duck.

   Ⓐ face   Ⓑ tail   Ⓒ bill

2. The platypus has _______ feet.

   Ⓐ three   Ⓑ webbed   Ⓒ thick

3. Platypus eggs feel like _______.

   Ⓐ fur   Ⓑ leather   Ⓒ mud

4. The platypus can live on _______ or in water.

   Ⓐ land   Ⓑ trees   Ⓒ rocks

5. The platypus and the spiny anteater are the only _______ that lay eggs.

   Ⓐ reptiles   Ⓑ birds   Ⓒ mammals

Word Analysis — Initial Consonant Blends

Say each picture name. Listen for the beginning sound. Write the letters that stand for the beginning sound.

1. ______atypus

2. ______og

3. ______ock

4. ______ess

5. ______ute

6. ______op

7. ______ake

8. ______ee

Choose one of the pictures above. Write a sentence using the name of that picture.

____

Say the word in dark print. Listen for the beginning sound. Read the sentence from the story. Circle the word in the sentence that has the same beginning sound as the word in dark print.

clock   Here are some clues.

stop   It stays in the water most of the time.

frog   But it's different from almost all other mammals.

Vocabulary — Synonyms

Synonyms are words that have the same or almost the same meanings. The words small and little are synonyms. Synonyms can help you find the meaning of a new word. Read these sentences.

The platypus is a mystery. It is a puzzle that surprises many people.

The words mystery and puzzle are both about the platypus. You know what a mystery is. The word mystery is a synonym for puzzle.

Read these sentences. Circle the synonym for the word in dark print.

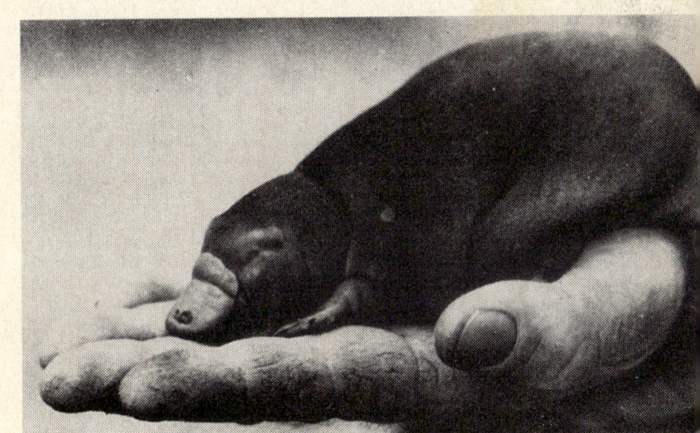

1. Mammals are the **same** in many ways. One way they are _____ is that they get milk from their mothers.

    different   alike

2. Many mammals have **fur**. It is the _____ that covers them.

    hair   nails

3. The platypus **story** is like a mystery. It is a _____ full of questions.

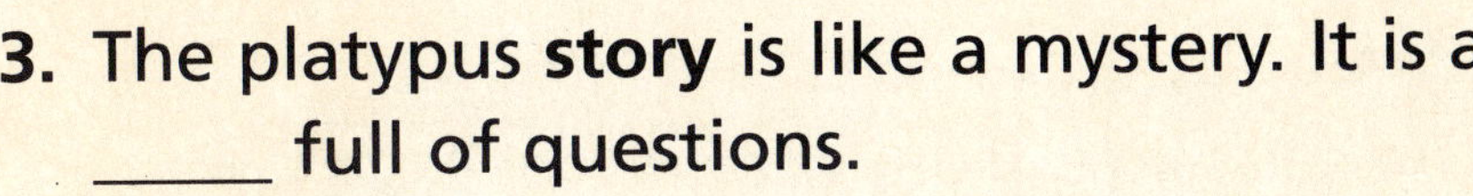

    animal   tale

Words That Were New to You

Choose words from the story that were new to you. Use a dictionary to check the meanings. Add the words and their meanings to your word list on page 127.

REREADING

Compare and Contrast

You can **compare** things to show how they are alike. You can **contrast** things to show how they are different.

Look at this diagram. It shows one way that the duck and platypus are alike. It shows one way that they are different.

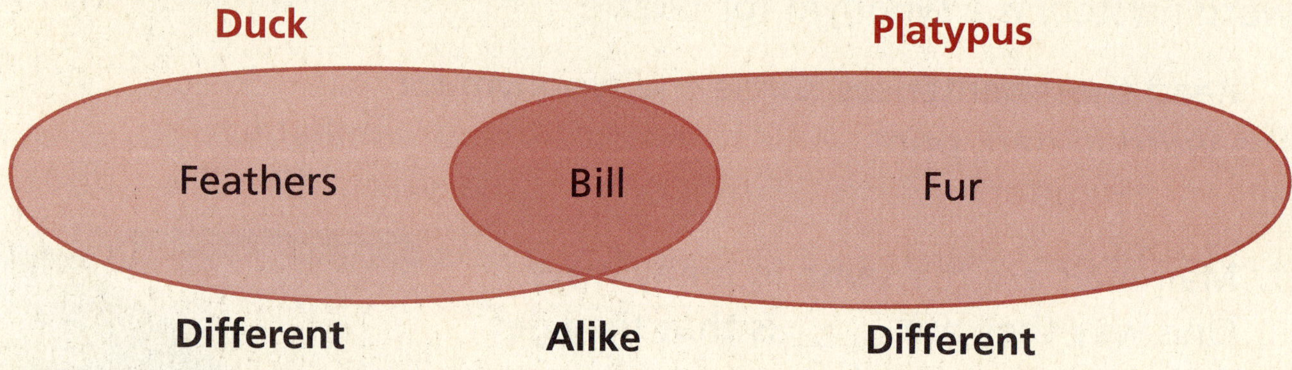

Reread the story. Look for other ways the duck and platypus are alike and different. Then finish this diagram.

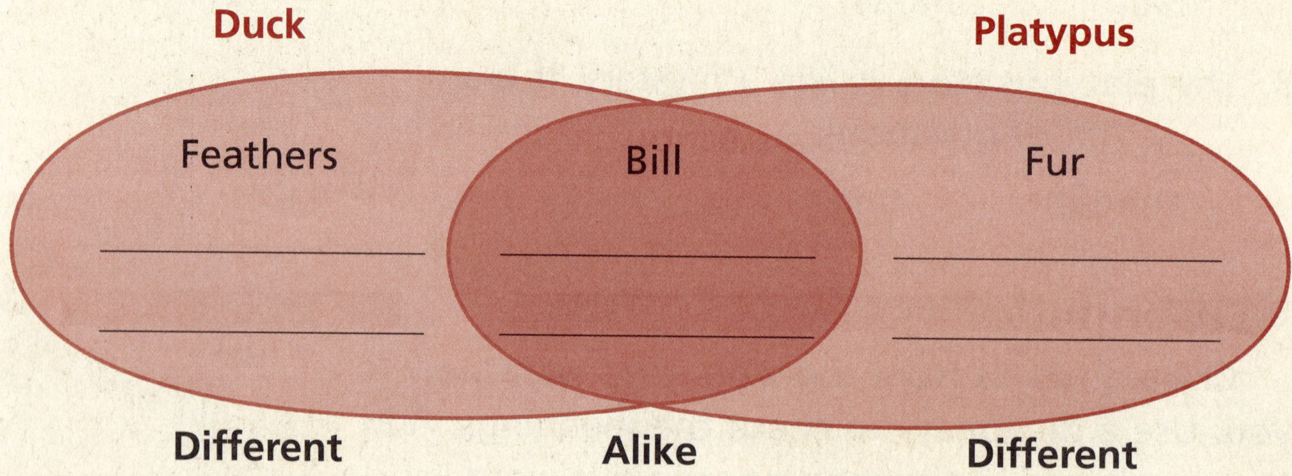

Drawing Conclusions

Writers don't always tell you everything. Sometimes you have to use story clues and what you already know to help you. That is called **drawing conclusions**. Read these sentences. Then circle the conclusion you would draw.

> A platypus has a bill like a duck. A platypus has webbed feet like a duck. A platypus has fur like a mammal.

1. A platypus is a strange animal.

2. A platypus sleeps during the day.

Use what you have learned to complete one of these activities.

1. Make a booklet telling people about the platypus. Find out more facts about it. Use an encyclopedia to help you.

2. Give the platypus a different name. Tell why you think it's a good name.

3. Imagine that there are only ten platypuses left in the world. What could you do to help the platypuses? Write a short paragraph about what you could do.

GETTING READY TO READ

You are going to read a mystery about two kids. They find something very special on the beach. Where will it lead them? What will they learn?

What Do You Think You Will Learn?

Look through "La Niña" on pages 55 through 58. Look at the pictures. What do you think the story will be about? Write your ideas below.

____

____

____

____

____

____

____

La Niña

Luis and Marta Garcia stood with their feet in the ocean water. They were digging in the wet sand with their toes.

Luis and Marta lived in Florida near the ocean. They were always looking for stuff in the water or on the beach.

"Look what I found!" Luis shouted. He pointed to something sticking out of the sand. "It's blue! I bet it's worth a lot of money."

Luis always thought that he found something worth a lot of money. This time he found an old blue shoe!

Suddenly, the sky turned dark. The wind began to roar. It was a sudden summer storm. Luis and Marta ran back to their house.

The storm lasted all night. But the next day was bright and sunny. Luis and Marta ate quickly and rushed to the beach. Big storms sometimes washed up great stuff!

The beach was full of seaweed and shells. But Luis found something hard and bumpy. It wasn't a shell.

"Look at this," he said to Marta. "There's some kind of writing on it. I bet it's worth a lot of money!"

"Just like that blue shoe," Marta laughed.

That night Luis showed Dad what he had found. Dad looked at it carefully.

"Can you take me to the spot where you found this?" Dad asked Luis.

The next day Luis took Dad and Marta to the spot. Dad noticed an old piece of wood that had washed up.

"Luis," Dad said. "I think you may have solved a 400 year old mystery!"

"What mystery?" Marta asked.

"About 400 years ago, a bad storm caused a Spanish treasure ship to sink in these waters. The ship's name was *La Niña*," Dad said.

"Treasure!" Luis yelled. "You mean gold coins and stuff?"

"Yes," Dad said. "But no one has been able to find *La Niña*. Until today, that is!"

"Look at this," Dad said, holding the piece of wood. "It has an *N* carved on it."

"*N* for *Niña*!" Marta shouted. "And Luis found a gold coin!"

"Maybe," Dad said. "We have to take it to a museum where people study old coins."

*   *   *

Thirty-five years later, Luis Garcia sat on the beach. He was telling the story of *La Niña* to his ten year old son.

"So Grandpa took the coin to a museum. And it was from *La Niña*!" he said. "It was a gold coin, and the museum people paid him for it. Many people came to our beach after that. Divers looked in the water. But no one ever found anything else. It's still a mystery!"

"Maybe I'll solve it," Luis's son said. "And it'll be worth a lot of money!"

Luis smiled as his son ran to the beach.

AFTER READING

What Did You Learn?

You have read "La Niña" for the first time. What did you think it would be about? Look back at page 54 to help you. What was the biggest surprise in this story? Write about it on the lines below.

____

____

____

Check Your Understanding

Read each sentence. Look at the words in the box. Choose one to complete each sentence. Write the word on the correct line.

coin	wood	ship	museum

1. *La Niña* was a Spanish treasure

   ______________________.

2. Luis found a ______________________ on the beach.

3. Dad found a piece of ______________________ with an *N* on it.

4. Dad took what Luis found to a

   ______________________.

Word Analysis — Final Consonant Blends

Say each picture name. Listen for the ending sound. Write the letters that stand for the ending sound.

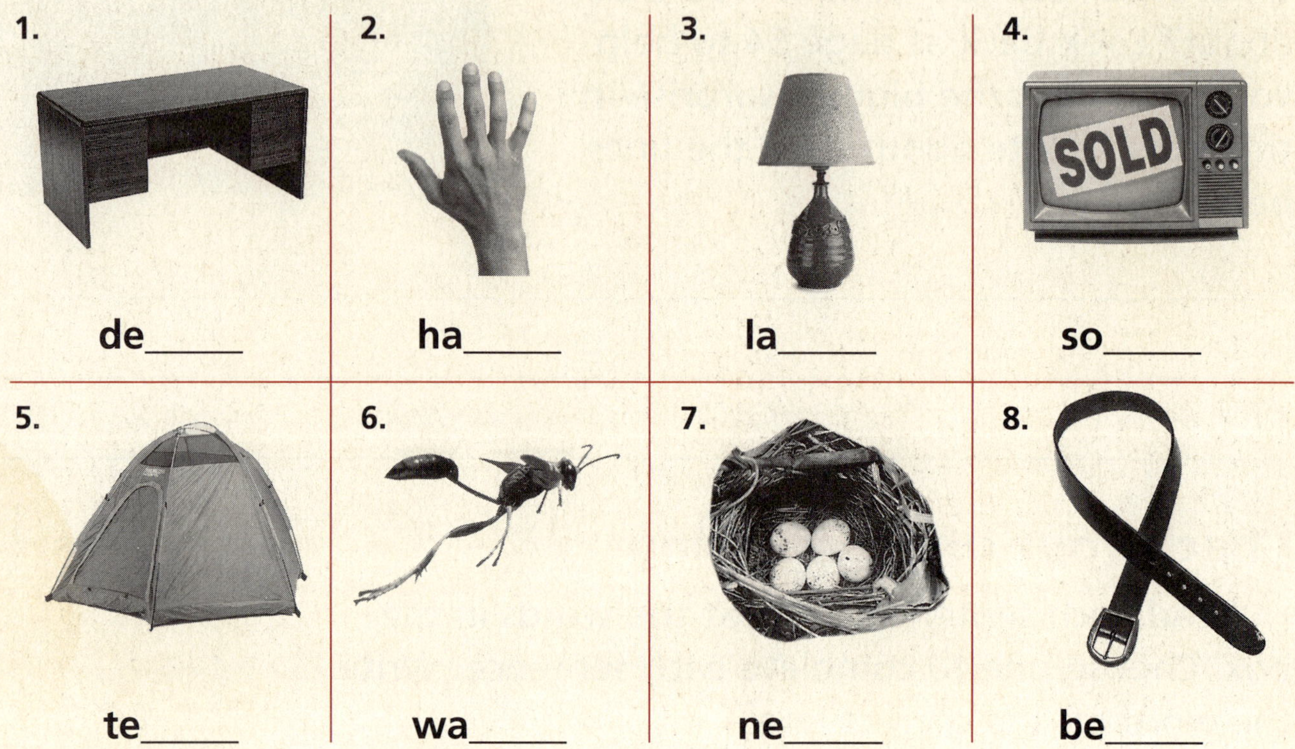

1.
de______

2.
ha______

3.
la______

4.
so______

5.
te______

6.
wa______

7.
ne______

8.
be______

Choose one of the pictures above. Write a sentence using the name of that picture.

____

Say the word in dark print. Listen for the ending sound. Read the sentence from the story. Circle the word in the sentence that has the same ending sound as the word in dark print.

hand   "There's some kind of writing on it."

gold   This time he found an old blue shoe.

Vocabulary — Contractions

Sometimes two words are put together to make a smaller word. The smaller word is called a **contraction**. An **apostrophe** takes the place of the missing letters in a contraction. An apostrophe looks like this **'**. Read this sentence from the story.

I bet it's worth a lot of money!

The word **it's** is a contraction. The word **it's** stands for **it is**. The apostrophe (') takes the place of the **i** in this contraction.

Read each sentence. Darken the circle next to the words that stand for each contraction in dark print.

1. Luis found something that **wasn't** a shell.

  Ⓐ was not   Ⓑ is not   Ⓒ would not

2. Marta **didn't** think it was worth anything.

  Ⓐ could not   Ⓑ did not   Ⓒ did have

3. Luis **hasn't** stopped telling about *La Niña*.

  Ⓐ will not   Ⓑ can not   Ⓒ has not

Words That Were New to You

Choose words from the story that were new to you. Use a dictionary to check the meanings. Add the words and their meanings to your word list on page 127.

REREADING

Cause and Effect

Sometimes one thing makes another thing happen. What happens is the called the **effect**. Why it happens is called the **cause**. Look at this sentence from the story.

> About 400 years ago, a bad storm caused a Spanish treasure ship to sink in these waters.

The ship sank is what happened. That is the effect. A bad storm is why it happened. That is the cause.

Reread "La Niña." Look for what happens in the story. Ask yourself why it happens. Then finish the cause and effect chart below.

Cause (Why did it happen?)	Effect (What happened?)
	Luis and Marta ran back to their house. (page 56)
	The ship sank. (page 57)
	People came to the beach. Divers looked in the water. (page 58)

Compare and Contrast

Luis found a shoe and a coin on the beach. Finish this diagram to show how these two finds were alike and how they were different.

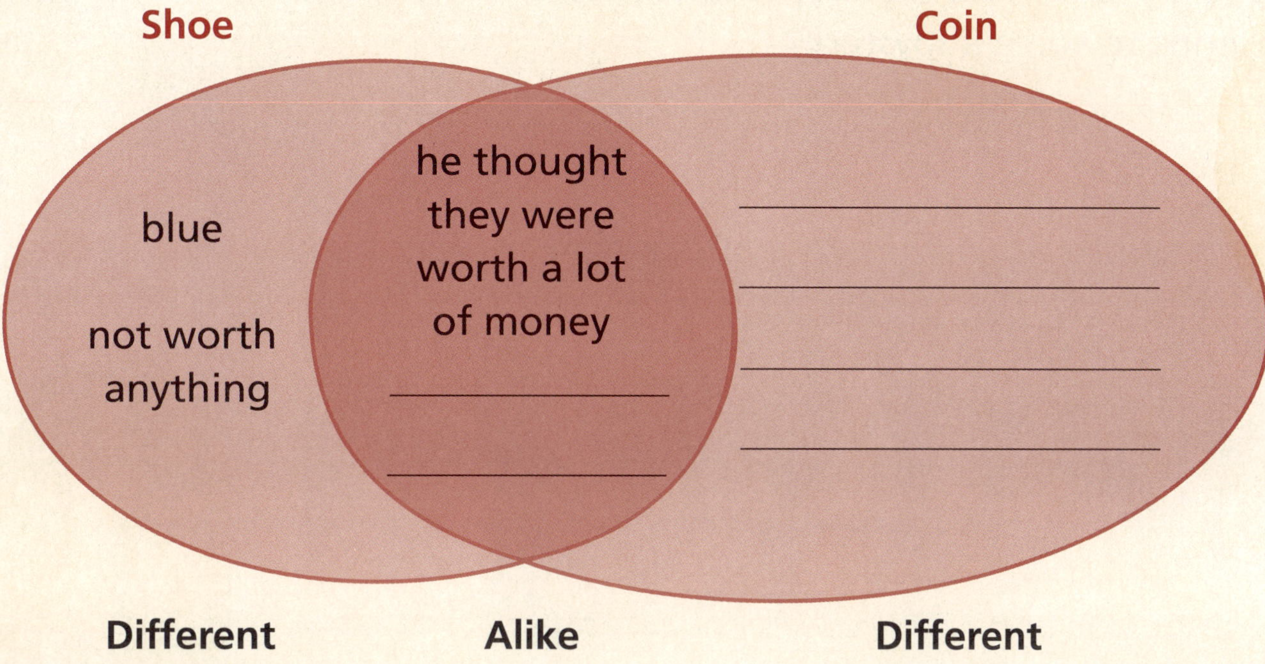

Think and Write

Use what you have learned to complete one of these activities.

1. Suppose you are a reporter. Write a story for your newspaper about Luis's discovery.

2. Imagine that you found the treasure of *La Niña*. Write a letter to a friend telling about it.

3. Suppose one of the sailors on *La Niña* kept a journal. What would it say? Write about it.

GETTING READY TO READ

The story you are going to read is called "The Mystery Kitten." It is about a group of children who try to solve a mystery. Did you ever work with friends to solve a mystery?

What Do You Think You Will Learn?

Look through "The Mystery Kitten" on pages 65 through 68. Look at the pictures. Think about the name of the story. What do you think you will find out when you read the story? Write your ideas below.

The Mystery Kitten

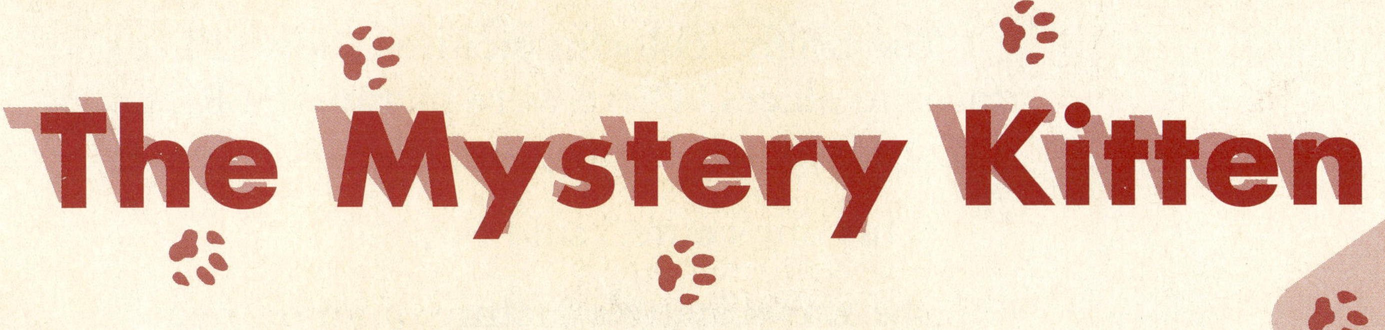

Lee's heart pounded. She raced up the stairs to Joey's apartment. Lee wanted to show her new camera to her friends. They were all waiting for her.

"Look what my grandma gave me for my birthday," Lee called. She held up the camera for everyone to see.

"I snapped pictures all day," Lee said. "I just got them from the one-hour film shop."

Lee pulled a pack of shiny snapshots from her bag. Then she passed them around.

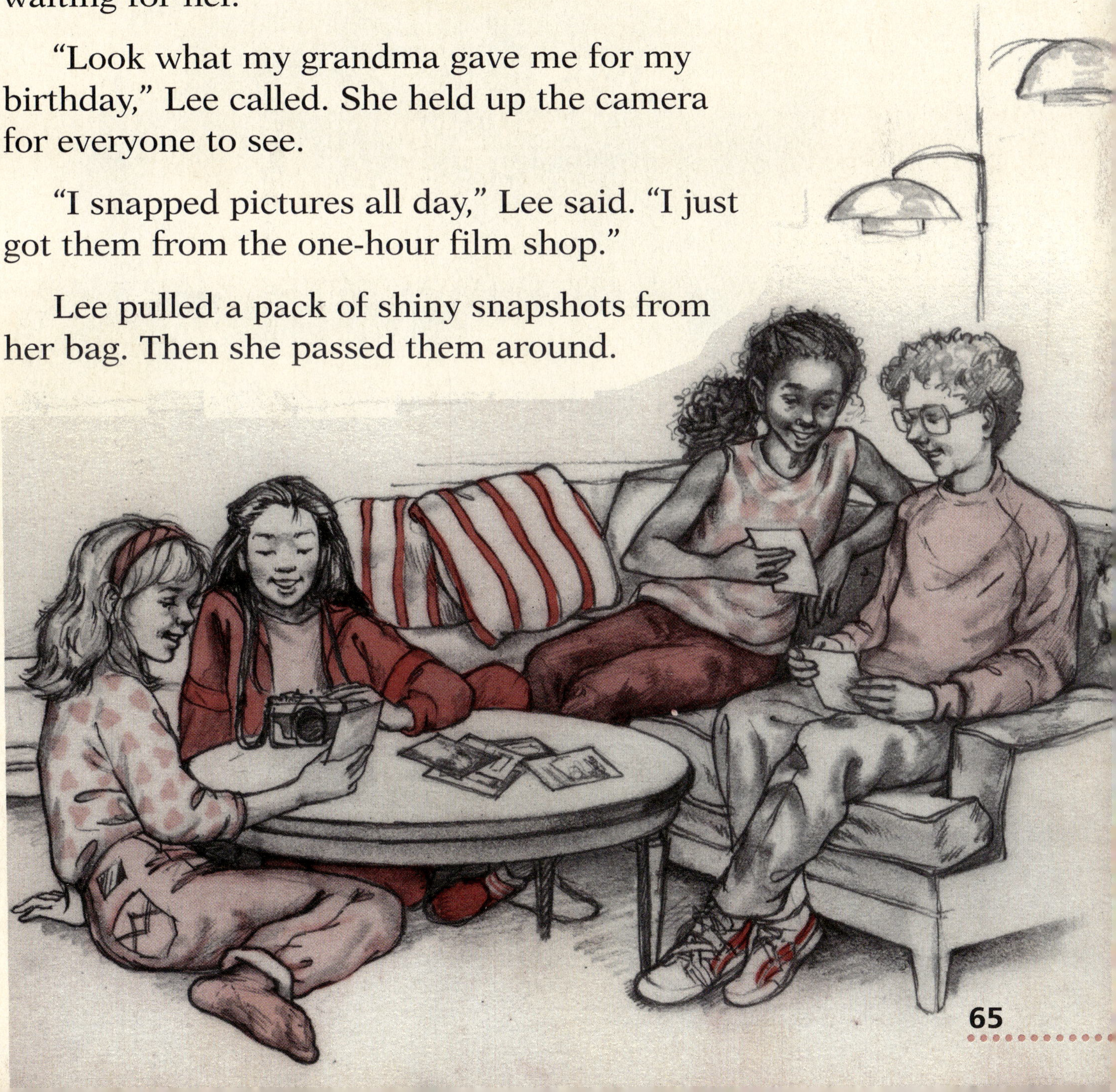

The bright, colorful pictures showed Lee's favorite places. There were pictures of Rick's Pizza Place, the library, and the youth center.

"This one's cute," said Bev.

She was waving a picture of an orange kitten. The kitten was sleeping on a bed. The clock by the bed said 1:05.

"Hey, I didn't take that picture!" said Lee. "I haven't seen any kittens today."

"Maybe someone used the camera!" said Joey.

"But who? And when?" asked Lee.

"We know it happened at 1:05," said Sue. "The only questions are who and where."

"I don't know where I was at 1:05," said Lee.

Bev had a plan. They could go back over Lee's path. Someone might remember her. They might know what time she had been there.

Soon the kids were at Rick's Pizza Place.

"I remember you," Rick told Lee. "You left here about 11:00."

"That's too early," Joey said.

Things weren't any better at the library. "You're the girl with the camera," said the woman who worked there. "You left at 12:40."

The last stop was the youth center. Lee found out she got there at 2:15.

"Why did it take you so long to get from the library to the youth center?" Bev asked.

"I went home for lunch," said Lee. "But I didn't take any pictures there."

"Let's check it out anyway," said Bev.

The kids went to Lee's house. They told her mom all about the mystery picture.

Mom smiled. Then she opened the bedroom door. An orange kitten walked through the door.

"It's the mystery kitten!" Bev cried.

"Happy birthday, Lee!" Mom said. "You left the camera in your room while you had lunch. I used it to take the kitten's picture."

Lee picked up the kitten and hugged it.

"What will you name her?" asked Sue.

Lee smiled, "I'll call her Mystery!"

AFTER READING

What Did You Learn?

You have read "The Mystery Kitten" for the first time. Look back on page 64. Was the mystery about what you thought it would be? What surprised you when you read the story? Write your answers on the lines below.

____

____

____

Check Your Understanding

Darken the circle next to the word that best completes each sentence.

1. Lee's grandma gave her a _______.

   Ⓐ camera   Ⓑ shirt   Ⓒ baseball

2. Bev found a picture of a _______.

   Ⓐ feather   Ⓑ kitten   Ⓒ toy

3. Rick was the man at the _______.

   Ⓐ library   Ⓑ park   Ⓒ pizza place

4. Lee's mom gave her a _______.

   Ⓐ kitten   Ⓑ camera   Ⓒ book

Word Analysis — Initial Consonant Digraphs

Words that begin with **sh** have the same beginning sound that you hear in the word shoe.

Words that begin with **wh** have the same beginning sound that you hear in the word whale.

Words that begin with **ch** have the same beginning sound that you hear in the word chair.

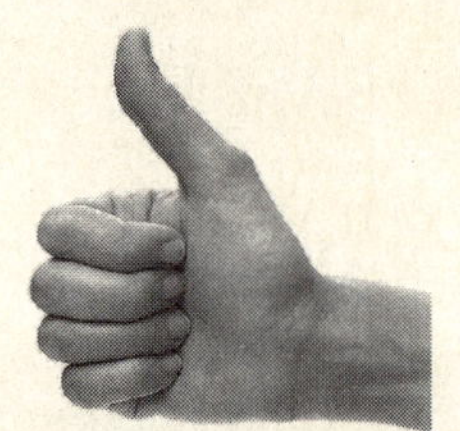

Words that begin with **th** have the same beginning sound that you hear in the word thumb.

Say the word in dark print. Listen for the beginning sound. Read the sentence from the story. Circle the word in each sentence that has the same beginning sound as the word in dark print.

shoe   She raced up the stairs to Joey's apartment.

whale   "I don't know where I was at 1:05," said Lee.

chair   "Let's check it out anyway," said Bev.

thumb   They were all waiting for her.

Vocabulary — Context Clues

When you see a word that is new to you, you can look at other words around it to help you find the meaning. Read these sentences from the story.

> Lee's heart pounded. She raced up
> the stairs to Joey's apartment.

You can figure out the meaning of pounded by looking at the words around it. You know that Lee was running up the stairs very fast. Her heart was probably beating very fast and very hard. So, pounded means "beat very hard and fast."

Find these words in the story. Look at the other words and sentences around them. Circle the meaning of the word.

1. camera (page 65)

something that takes pictures

something that makes rings

2. snapshots (page 65)

cards   pictures

3. apartment (page 65)

place to live   place to see a doctor

Words That Were New to You

Choose words from the story that were new to you. Use a dictionary to check their meanings. Add the words and their meanings to your word list on page 127.

REREADING

Dialogue

When people say things in a story, the words are called **dialogue**. You can tell when there is dialogue because the words have special marks around them. The marks look like this **" "**. They are called **quotation marks**. Read this sentence.

"Happy birthday, Lee!" Mom said.

The quotation marks are a clue that someone is saying Happy birthday, Lee. The writer tells you that it is Mom who is talking.

Read the story again. Look for clues that tell you when someone is talking. Then read the sentences below. Look back in the story to find who said them. Write that person's name on the line.

1. "Look what my grandma gave me for my birthday." (page 65)

   ____

2. "Maybe someone used the camera!" (page 66) _______________________

3. "You left here about 11:00." (page 67) _______________________

4. "Let's check it out anyway." (page 68)

   ____

Cause and Effect

Sometimes one thing makes another thing happen. What happens is the **effect**. Why it happens is the **cause**. Finish the cause and effect chart. Use the story to help you.

Cause (Why did it happen?)	Effect (What happened?)
	The woman at the library remembered Lee. (page 67)
	It took Lee a long time to get from the library to the youth center. (page 68)
	The kitten walked out. (page 68)

THINK and WRITE

Use what you have learned to complete one of these activities.

1. Imagine what Joey and Lee might tell each other after the story is over. Write what they might say.

2. Pretend that you are Lee. Tell Grandma about the kitten. Write some questions Grandma might ask. Write the answers you would give.

3. Make a birthday card for Lee. Write her a mystery birthday wish.

GETTING READY TO READ

The last story in this unit is "A Nature Mystery." It is about someone who solves mysteries. What kind of mysteries do you think the person solves?

What Do You Think You Will Learn?

Look through "A Nature Mystery" on pages 75 through 78. Look at the pictures. What do you think you will learn as you read this story? Write your ideas below.

____

____

____

____

A NATURE MYSTERY

Some people spend their lives solving mysteries. They may find out how something happened. They may track down missing people. This story is about someone who solves mysteries in nature. It is about Dr. Jane Goodall.

Dr. Jane Goodall is a scientist who studies animals. She studies the things that animals do. Dr. Goodall studies many different kinds of animals. But she has studied chimpanzees the most. Chimpanzees are also called chimps.

Dr. Jane Goodall has learned many things about chimpanzees.

Jane Goodall grew up in England. She always loved animals. She liked to watch them all the time. She saw how they lived. She took notes about the animals.

When Jane Goodall was 23 years old, she went to Africa. She met Dr. Louis Leakey. He was a great scientist. He studied old bones. Jane Goodall helped Dr. Leakey with his work. She helped him for a few years.

Jane Goodall loved her work with Dr. Leakey. She loved to be around wild animals in Africa, too. She wanted to learn more about the animals.

Learning about wild animals would not be easy. She would have to watch them all the time. She would have to get very close to them. What if the animals got scared? They might run away. They might even try to hurt her! But Jane Goodall still wanted to learn about them.

In 1960 Jane Goodall got her wish. She got to study animals in the wild. People didn't know much about chimps in those days. They wanted to know more about how chimps live in the wild. Jane Goodall could study chimps. She could live with them in Africa. She could help solve the mystery.

Every day Dr. Goodall followed the chimps around. At first they stayed away from her. Some of them hid in the treetops. After a while, though, they let her get closer.

Dr. Goodall watched the chimps. She watched the way that the chimps acted. She listened to the sounds they made. She watched them eat. She watched them drink. She even watched them at nighttime.

Dr. Goodall wrote down everything that the chimpanzees did. That way she would remember everything that she saw and heard.

Chimpanzees take care of each other.

Soon the chimps were used to having Dr. Goodall around. She even made friends with some of them. She gave them names.

Dr. Goodall learned a lot about chimpanzees. She found out that they hold hands, hug, and even kiss. Dr. Goodall learned that chimps can get very angry, too. An angry chimp might throw a rock. The chimp might stomp around or scream!

Dr. Goodall also solved another mystery. Most people thought that chimps just ate vegetables, fruits, and small animals. But Dr. Goodall found out that they were wrong. Chimps eat big animals, too. They even eat pigs!

Dr. Goodall stayed in Africa for many years. She studied baboons, monkeys, hyenas, and other animals. Dr. Jane Goodall has helped solve some of nature's mysteries.

AFTER READING

What Did You Learn?

You have just read "A Nature Mystery" for the first time. Did you learn the things you thought you would learn? Look back at what you wrote on page 74. What was the most interesting thing you learned? Write your answers below.

____

____

____

Check Your Understanding

Read each sentence. Look at the words in the box. Choose one to complete each sentence. Write the correct word on the line.

chimps	Africa	fruits	scientists

1. Dr. Goodall began to study _______________ in 1960.

2. Dr. Goodall and Dr. Leakey are

   both _______________.

3. Chimps eat vegetables, _______________, and animals.

4. Dr. Goodall worked with Dr. Leakey in

   _______________.

Word Analysis — Final Consonant Digraphs

Words that end with **sh** have the same sound that you hear at the end of the word **brush**.

Words that end with **ck** have the same sound that you hear at the end of the word **sock**.

Words that end with **nk** have the same sound that you hear at the end of the word **sink**.

Words that end with **ng** have the same sound that you hear at the end of the word **ring**.

Say the word in dark print. Listen for the ending sound. Read the sentence from the story. Circle the word in the sentence that has the same ending sound as the word in dark print.

brush   In 1960 Jane Goodall got her wish.

sock   An angry chimp might throw a rock.

sink   She watched them drink.

ring   Dr. Goodall wrote down everything that the chimpanzees did.

Vocabulary — Compound Words

Sometimes two smaller words can be put together to make one larger word. The larger word is called a **compound word**. Look at this sentence.

Jane Goodall wrote about chimps in her notebook.

The word notebook is a compound word. It is made up of two smaller words. Think about what each word means. You can figure out that notebook means "a book of notes."

Read each sentence. Darken the circle next to the words that best tell the meaning of the compound word in dark print.

1. Some chimps like to hide in the **treetops**.

   Ⓐ tops of chimps   Ⓑ tops of trees   Ⓒ tops of rocks

2. Dr. Goodall watched the chimps at **nighttime**.

   Ⓐ time of day   Ⓑ time of eating   Ⓒ time of night

3. Dr. Goodall liked to get up at **sunrise**.

   Ⓐ when the sun rises

   Ⓑ when the sun goes down

   Ⓒ when the moon rises

Words That Were New to You

Choose words from the story that were new to you. Use a dictionary to check the meanings. Add the words and their meanings to your word list on page 127.

REREADING

Main Idea and Details

The **main idea** is the most important idea in a paragraph. It tells what a paragraph is all about. **Details** tell the reader more about the main idea. Read this paragraph from "A Nature Mystery."

> Soon the chimps were used to having Dr. Goodall around. She even made friends with some of them. She gave them names.

The first sentence tells the main idea. The other sentences tell more about the main idea.

Reread "A Nature Mystery." Look for sentences that tell what each paragraph is about. Then, look for details that tell more about the main idea.

After you reread "A Nature Mystery," write two details that tell more about each main idea below.

1. Main Idea: Learning about wild animals would not be easy. (page 76)

DETAIL: ____

DETAIL: ____

2. Main Idea: Dr. Goodall learned a lot about chimpanzees. (page 78)

DETAIL: ____

DETAIL: ____

Sequence

It is important to know the order in which things happen in a story. Read these sentences. Write 1, 2, or 3 before each sentence.

______ Dr. Goodall helped Dr. Louis Leakey with his work.

______ Dr. Goodall made friends with the chimpanzees.

______ Dr. Goodall went to Africa.

THINK and WRITE

Use what you have learned to complete one of these activities.

1. Imagine you are making a TV show about Jane Goodall. Write what you would say. Tell what pictures you would show.

2. A baboon is another kind of animal that Dr. Goodall studied. Find out about baboons in the encyclopedia or other books in the library. Write two facts about them.

3. What kind of animal would you like to study? Write about it.

4. Find out more about Jane Goodall. Write a short report.

5. Think of another nature mystery. How would you go about solving it? Tell about your ideas.

BIG AND LITTLE

What is big and what is little?

You get used to thinking of things as certain sizes. Worms and spoons are small. Buildings and monsters are big. In this unit, you will read about worms as long as tall buildings. You will learn about monsters not even one foot tall. You will see how big can be small and small can be big. Strange things are often the most interesting!

What Do You Already Know?

Think of all the things you know that are bigger or smaller than you. What's the biggest thing you've ever seen? What's the smallest thing you've ever seen? Write about these things.

____

____

____

____

____

What Do You Want to Find Out?

In this unit you will find out about big and little things. What would you like to find out about big and little things? On the lines below, write some questions you want answered. You may find the answers to your questions as you read.

____

____

____

____

____

____

____

GETTING READY TO READ

The first story you will read is "Animals Come in All Sizes." What do you know about very big or very small animals? What do you think it would be like to see some of these animals?

What Do You Think You Will Learn?

Look through "Animals Come in All Sizes" on pages 87 through 90. Look at the pictures. Read the headings. What do you think you will learn when you read this story? Write your ideas below.

____

____

____

____

____

Animals Come in All Sizes

How long is a worm? Earthworms are only about as long as one of your fingers. But have you ever seen a ribbon worm? The ribbon worm lives in the sea. If you held one end of the ribbon worm out the window of an 18-story building, the other end would reach the ground!

Why do you think this worm is called a ribbon worm?

You've probably seen spiders. But one spider is so small you would have a hard time seeing it at all. The Samoan spider is smaller than the dot over the letter *i*.

Uh, Oh — That's Big!

The Chilean red-leg spider is much larger than the Samoan spider. Its body is the size of your hand! The Chilean red-leg spider is so big, it eats mice and small birds.

The goliath frog can jump 10 feet in a single leap.

You might think of a frog as a small animal. But wait until you see the goliath frog! The goliath frog has a head as wide as a small plate. Each eye is the size of a gumball. Its front legs are almost the size of a baby's arm. And its back legs are even bigger.

Goliath frogs have rows of sharp teeth in their mouths. They catch bugs and smaller frogs to eat!

Small Time

One frog that a goliath could eat is the tiny tree frog. This frog is so small it can hide on a leaf. Its tiny size makes a tree frog hard to find.

Tree frogs do something else that makes them hard to find. Tree frogs can change their color to look like whatever they are near. When they're hiding in the leaves, tree frogs turn bright green. When they're hiding on tree bark, these tiny frogs turn brown. This way, even the tiniest frog can hide from bigger animals that want to eat it!

This tree frog is hidden from other animals.

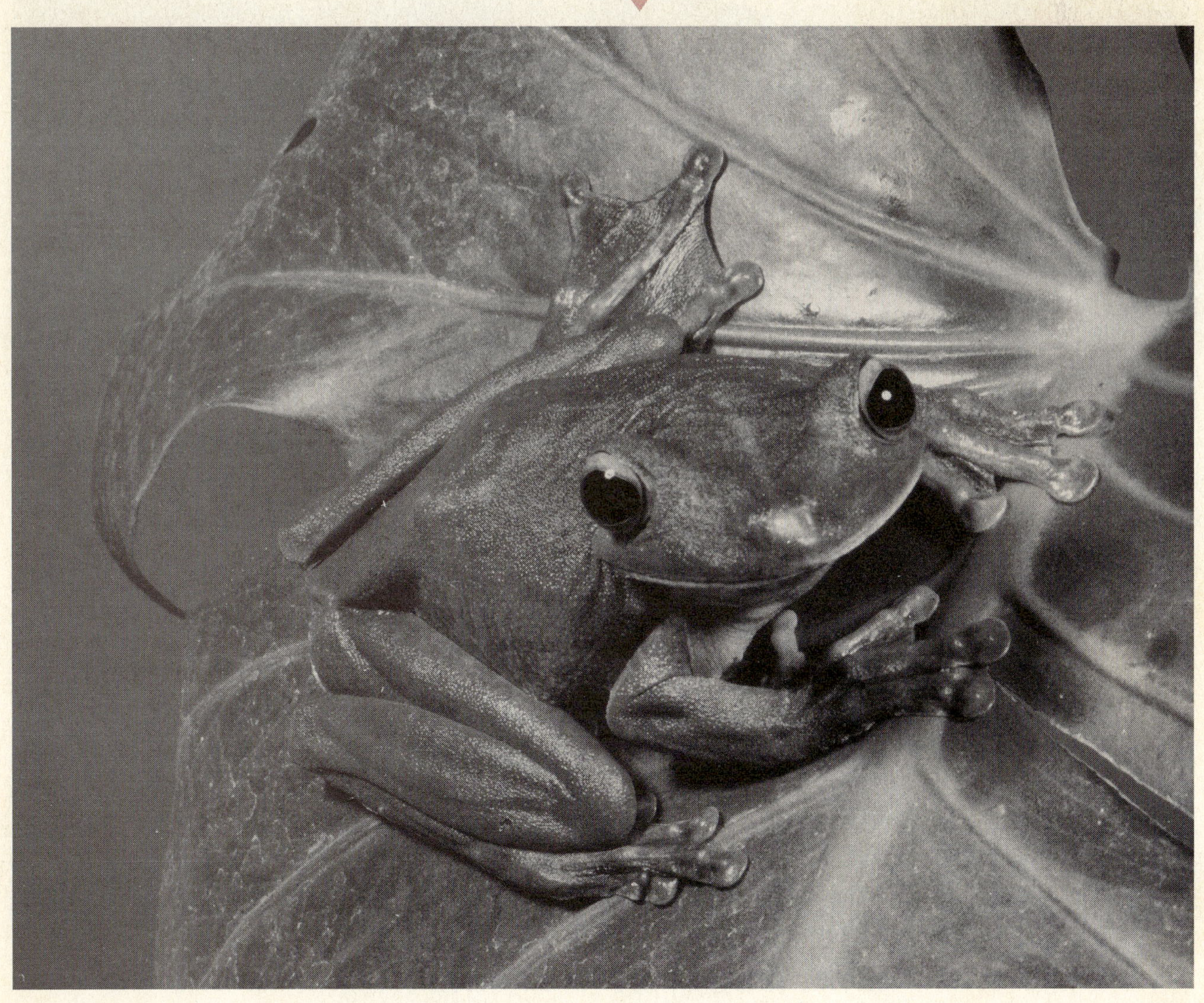

The frilled lizard can look like a monster!

A Small Monster

The frilled lizard of Australia looks like a monster. But for a monster, it's pretty small. The frilled lizard only stands about one foot tall. When it stands up, it would not even reach your knee.

The frilled lizard has a flap of loose skin around its neck. When the lizard is frightened, it pushes out the folds of skin. This makes the lizard look much larger. Then it opens its mouth and shows its teeth. Even bigger animals are afraid of it.

Now you know about some big animals and some small ones, too. Which kind would you like to know more about?

AFTER READING

What Did You Learn?

You have read "Animals Come in All Sizes" for the first time. Now look back at what you wrote on page 86. Did you learn what you thought you would learn? What were you surprised to learn? Write your answers below.

____

____

____

Check Your Understanding

Darken the circle next to the word that best completes each sentence.

1. The ribbon worm is very long and lives in the _____.

   Ⓐ trees   Ⓑ grass   Ⓒ sea

2. The Chilean red-leg spider is a _____ spider.

   Ⓐ friendly   Ⓑ large   Ⓒ small

3. The goliath frog has a head as wide as a small _____.

   Ⓐ hand   Ⓑ plate   Ⓒ gumball

4. When the frilled lizard is frightened, it pushes out the folds of its _____.

   Ⓐ skin   Ⓑ feathers   Ⓒ wings

Word Analysis — R-Controlled Vowels

You know about the long sound of vowels. You also know about the short sound of vowels. There is another vowel sound. It is the sound a vowel makes if it comes before the letter r. Say each picture name. Listen to the vowel sound.

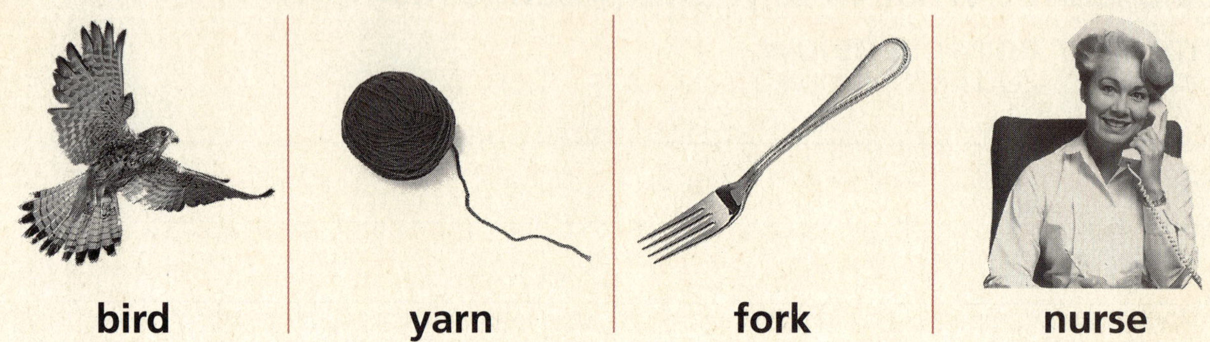

bird   yarn   fork   nurse

Choose one of the pictures above. Write a sentence using the picture name.

____

____

Say the word in dark print. Listen for the vowel sound. Read each sentence about the story. Circle the word in the sentence that has the same vowel sound as the word in dark print.

nurse   Tree frogs can turn bright green.

bird   A tree frog might turn brown in the dirt.

yarn   Tree frogs hide on tree bark.

fork   The frilled lizard is very short.

Vocabulary — Multiple Meanings

Some words have more than one meaning. The word bark can mean "the sound a dog makes." It can also mean "the covering of a tree." Read this sentence from the story.

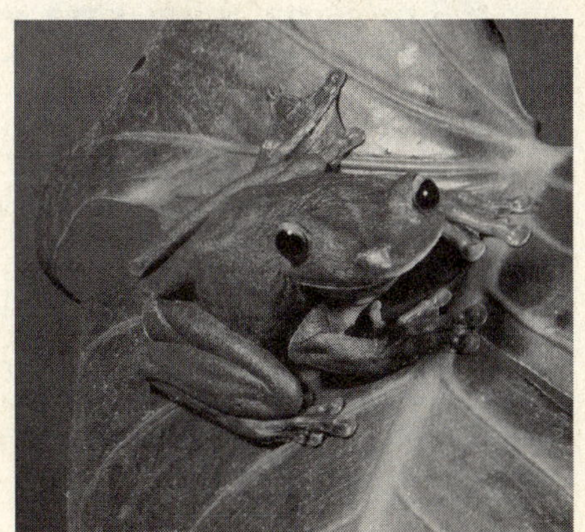

> **When they're hiding on tree bark, these tiny frogs turn brown.**

To tell the meaning of bark here, look at the other words in the sentence. The word tree is a clue. It helps you tell that in this sentence, bark means "the covering of a tree."

Read the sentences below. Circle the meaning of each word in dark print.

1. The Samoan spider is smaller than the dot over the **letter** *i*.

   piece of mail   part of the alphabet

2. Goliath frogs have **rows** of sharp teeth in their mouths.

   lines   uses oars

3. Tree frogs can **change** their color to look like whatever they are near.

   coins   become different

Words That Were New to You

Choose words from the story that were new to you. Use a dictionary to check the meanings. Add the words and their meanings to your word list on page 128.

REREADING

Drawing Conclusions

Writers don't always tell the reader everything. Sometimes you have to use story clues to help you. This is called **drawing conclusions**. Read this paragraph.

> The goliath frog has a head as wide as a small plate. Each eye is the size of a gumball. Its front legs are almost the size of a baby's arm.

The writer doesn't tell you how big the goliath frog is. But you can make a good guess about it. You can draw the conclusion that the goliath frog is very big.

Look for story clues. Use them to draw conclusions. You will better understand what you read.

Reread "Animals Come in All Sizes." Use what you know and clues in the story to help you finish each sentence. Circle the best answer. Then write one story clue that helped you.

1. The goliath frog

   can jump far.   cannot jump far.   can sing.

   CLUE: _______________________________________

2. The tree frog does not

   eat bugs.   weigh very much.   jump.

   CLUE: _______________________________________

Main Idea and Details

A **main idea** tells what a paragraph is all about. **Details** tell more about the main idea. Write a detail about each main idea. Use the story to help you.

1. Main Idea: The Chilean red-leg spider is much larger than the Samoan spider. (page 88)

DETAIL: ____________________________

2. Main Idea: Tree frogs can change their color to look like whatever they are near. (page 89)

DETAIL: ____________________________

THINK and WRITE

Use what you have learned to complete one of these activities.

1. Find out more about spiders. Use the encyclopedia and other books to help you. Share your findings with the class.

2. Pretend that you discovered a new animal. It can be a big animal or a small animal. Draw a picture of it. Give it a name and tell about it.

3. Pretend you are one of the animals in the story. You've just seen a human being for the first time. Write what a human being looks like to that animal.

GETTING READY TO READ

The next story you are going to read is "Big News!" Can you think of something big that people have made? If you could make something really big, what would it be?

What Do You Think You Will Learn?

Look through "Big News!" on pages 97 through 100. Look at the pictures. What do you think you will learn when you read this story? Write your ideas below.

____

____

____

____

____

BIG NEWS!

You have read about animals that are bigger than usual. People have made things that are bigger than usual, too. Would you like to sleep under a blanket bigger than two football fields? Keep reading to find out about more "biggies"!

On a Roll!

Have you ever been on a roller coaster? One of the world's biggest roller coasters is in Busch Gardens in Tampa, Florida. The roller coaster is called Kumba. As the ride begins, people hold their breath. The car climbs slowly up. It goes to the top of a hill 14 stories high. Then, it zooms down to the ground going 63 miles an hour! Screams fill the air! Back up again. Down, up, around. It even turns upside down seven times!

The ride on Kumba thrills people day after day.

Another giant roller coaster is Batman. This one is at Six Flags Great America in Illinois. Batman is ten stories high. It moves up slowly. It loops and turns and climbs. Then it races straight down at 50 miles an hour. Batman is no place for weak hearts! Some people say it's like flying.

Toyland

Maybe you'd rather stay on the ground and go shopping. You could visit Hamleys in London, England. This store is the biggest toy store in the world. It covers six big floors. There are about 50,000 different toys sold at Hamleys. The largest is a giant stuffed toy rhinoceros. The smallest toy is a teacup for a doll's house.

The giant toy teddy bear welcomes children to Hamleys.

A Very Big Truck Stop

All over the country, truck drivers bring food and other things to stores. They stop to get gas and sometimes food at places called truck stops. Most truck stops have a few gas pumps, a place to eat, and a place to sleep. But there is one that is very different! It is called the Giant Travel Center. It was built 120 miles west of Albuquerque, New Mexico, in 1987.

The Giant Travel Center was built for truck drivers. But today, people from all over stop by to see one of the biggest truck stops in the world. The Giant Travel Center has a 35-acre parking lot and 26 gas pumps! There's even a bus to take people from the parking lot to the main building.

The main building is filled with things to do. You can go to a movie. Or you can shop at one of the nine stores in the mini-mall. You can even wash your clothes!

The Biggest Piggy Bank

Penny the Pig is 6 feet 11 inches tall. She is as tall as a basketball player. Penny is 10 feet wide and 17 feet long. Penny the Pig can hold a lot of pennies! And the money put in her is used to help the homeless.

The Biggest Blanket

The members of a knitting club made the biggest blanket in the world. The blanket was made in 1993 in England. It is big enough to cover two football fields.

The Biggest Float

Everyone loves a parade! And everyone loves to watch the floats roll by. These big, flat wagons can be very large. The largest one was made by the World of Dreams Foundation in Montreal, Canada. This float was almost 185 feet long.

AFTER READING

What Did You Learn?

You have just read "Big News!" for the first time. Now look back at what you wrote on page 96. Did you learn what you thought you would learn? What were you surprised to learn? Write your answers below.

____

____

Check Your Understanding

Read each sentence. Look at the words in the box. Choose one to complete each sentence. Write the word on the correct line.

coasters	truck	Hamleys	Batman

1. Kumba is one of the biggest roller

   ___________________ in the world.

2. Another giant roller coaster is

   ___________________ in Illinois.

3. The largest toy store is ___________________
   in England.

4. The Giant Travel Center is a

   ___________________ stop.

Word Analysis — Vowel Digraphs ea
(long e and short e)

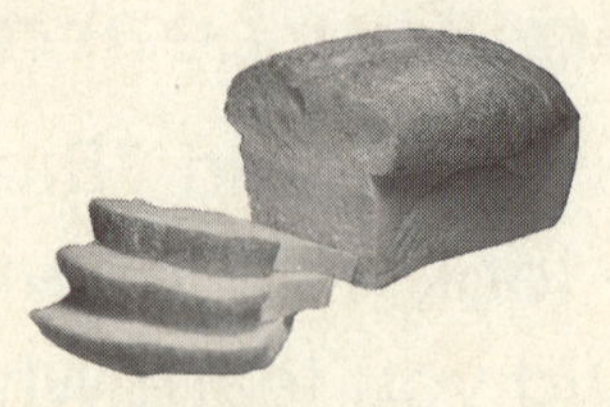

In some words the vowels ea have the **long e** sound that you hear in the word leaf.

In some words the vowels ea have the **short e** sound that you hear in the word bread.

One way to tell which sound ea stands for is to say the word out loud. Try both sounds. Listen for the sound that helps make a word.

Say each picture name. Listen for the vowel sound. Circle the words that have the same vowel sound.

1. 

leaf

head
tea
teach
spread

2.

bread

dream
dead
team
thread

Read this sentence from the story. Circle the word that has the **long e** sound that you hear in leaf.

3. The smallest toy is a teacup for a doll's house.

Read this sentence from the story. Circle the word that has the **short e** sound that you hear in bread.

4. As the ride begins, people hold their breath.

Vocabulary — Antonyms

Words that have opposite meanings are called antonyms. The words big and small are antonyms. Read these sentences.

> **The roller coaster goes to the top of the hill. Then it zooms down to the bottom.**

The words top and bottom are antonyms. If you know what top means, you can figure out from the sentences that bottom has the opposite meaning.

Read these sentences. Darken the circle next to the antonym of the word in dark print.

1. The stuffed rhinoceros is the **biggest** toy at Hamleys. The teacup is the _____ toy.

   Ⓐ smallest   Ⓑ nicest   Ⓒ fattest

2. The track on this roller coaster is **straight**. It isn't twisted and _____.

   Ⓐ smooth   Ⓑ tall   Ⓒ curved

3. The Batman roller coaster moves up the track **slowly**. Then it races down very _____ at 50 miles an hour!

   Ⓐ scary   Ⓑ quickly   Ⓒ high

Words That Were New to You

Choose words from the story that were new to you. Use a dictionary to check the meanings. Add the words and their meanings to your word list on page 128.

REREADING

Referents

A **noun** is the name of a person, place, or thing. A **pronoun** can take the place of a noun in a sentence. The words in the box below are pronouns.

I	he	she	they	we	it	you

Read these sentences.

> As the ride begins, the car climbs slowly up. It goes to the top of a hill.

The word **car** is a noun. The word **it** is a pronoun. The pronoun **it** stands for the noun **car**.

Read these sentences. Look at the pronoun in dark print. Circle the noun that each pronoun stands for.

1. Kumba is a very big roller coaster. **It** thrills people.

2. Children love Hamleys. **They** visit all the time.

3. Penny is a big pig. **She** is not real.

Reread "Big News!" Then look at page 100. Find one place where a pronoun stands for a noun. Write the sentences on the lines below. Underline the noun. Circle the pronoun.

____

____

Drawing Conclusions

Writers don't always tell you everything that is happening in a story. You may have to use story clues and what you already know to help you.

Use what you know and clues in the story to help you finish the sentence. Circle the best answer. Then write one story clue that helped you.

1. The Batman roller coaster is very _______.

   scary   slow   small

   CLUE: ____

THINK and WRITE

Use what you have learned to complete one of these activities.

1. Pretend that you can go to see one of the big things from the story. What would you want to see? Write a journal entry about it.

2. Draw a path for a roller coaster. Show how many loops and upside-down turns you would have. Tell about it.

3. Suppose you could build something very, very big. What would it be? What would it do? What would you call it? Write a paragraph telling about your idea.

GETTING READY TO READ

You are about to read "Movie Magic." Think about movies you have seen. Did you ever see a movie about a person who got very, very small? Did you ever see a movie about a person who got very, very tall? Which movie did you like best?

What Do You Think You Will Learn?

Look through "Movie Magic" on pages 107 through 110. Look at the pictures. What do you think you will learn when you read this story? Write your ideas below.

____

____

____

____

____

Movie Magic

Sometimes it's hard to believe the size of things in the movies. A person can look as tall as a mountain or as tiny as an ant.

You know that people cannot really be that big or small. But did you ever wonder how the movie makers do that? Here is how they did it in two movies you might have seen.

These kids look like small toys in the movie *Honey, I Blew Up the Kid*.

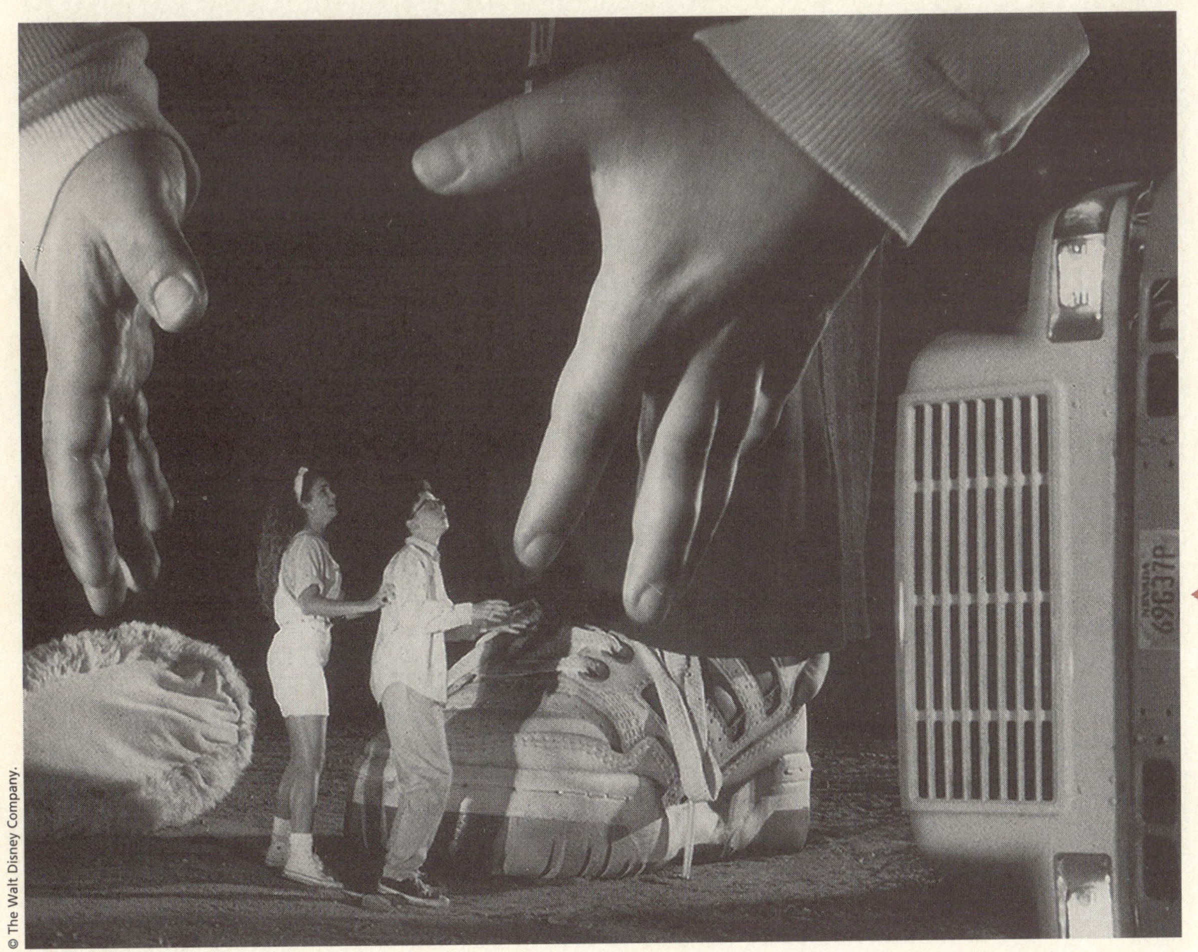

The movie *Honey, I Shrunk the Kids* is about a man who makes a big mistake. He shrinks three kids. He makes them smaller than they were before.

The kids end up small enough to fit on the end of your finger. Imagine being that small. Even crossing a backyard could be very scary.

Making the kids look small was not easy. Movie makers found a way to do it. They made everything around the kids very big. They built giant tables and chairs. They made huge forks and spoons. They even built a giant fly. When real kids stood next to these huge things, the kids looked tiny.

This boy looks smaller than a spoon!

Some parts of the movie were tricky to make.
In one part the kids have to get across a puddle.
It's just a small puddle in the yard. But that
puddle is like a giant lake for tiny kids. The movie
makers had a smart way to make it look real.

First, the movie makers had to get 13,000
pounds of dirt. Then, they mixed the dirt with
water to make more than 25,000 gallons of
mud! The mud turned into a huge puddle.
Finally, they filmed the kids crossing the giant
puddle. It was messy, but it worked! The kids
looked very, very small.

Now you know how movies can make
people look tiny. Can you guess how they can
make people look like giants?

This make-believe fly is huge. That's why the kids look so small.

In the movie *Honey, I Blew Up the Kid*, a baby is larger than a nine-story building. The movie makers used special tricks to make the baby look so big. First, they built very tiny buildings. Then, they put the baby next to the buildings. Finally, they took pictures of the baby next to the tiny buildings. In the movie, the baby looks huge next to the tiny buildings!

When you watch the movie, you see a giant baby walking down a city street. The baby looks much bigger than the buildings!

© The Walt Disney Company

So now you know some of the secrets that movie makers use to make things look big or small. It may be hard to believe. But it's still fun to pretend that it's all real.

After Reading

What Did You Learn?

You have read "Movie Magic" for the first time. Now look back at what you wrote on page 106. Did you learn what you thought you would learn? What were you surprised to learn? Write your answers on the lines below.

____

____

____

Check Your Understanding

Darken the circle next to the word that best completes each sentence.

1. To make kids look very small, movie makers made everything around them look ______.

   Ⓐ small   Ⓑ fat   Ⓒ big

2. In *Honey, I Shrunk the Kids*, the movie makers built giant tables, chairs, ______, and spoons.

   Ⓐ forks   Ⓑ kids   Ⓒ buildings

3. The mud puddle in *Honey, I Shrunk the Kids* looks like a giant ______.

   Ⓐ bowl   Ⓑ lake   Ⓒ rock

4. The kid in *Honey, I Blew Up the Kid* looks big because the buildings around him are really ______.

   Ⓐ tall   Ⓑ tiny   Ⓒ red

Word Analysis — Vowel Digraphs ie (long e and long i)

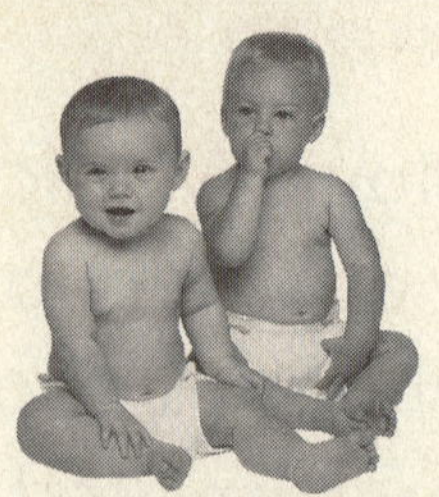

In some words the vowels **ie** have the **long i** sound that you hear in the word **tie**.

In some words the vowels **ie** have the **long e** sound that you hear in the word **babies**.

One way to tell which sound **ie** stands for is to say the word out loud. Try both sounds. Listen for the sound that helps make a word.

Say each picture name. Listen for the vowel sound. Circle the words that have the same vowel sound.

1. 

pie

thief

tried

believe

tie

2. 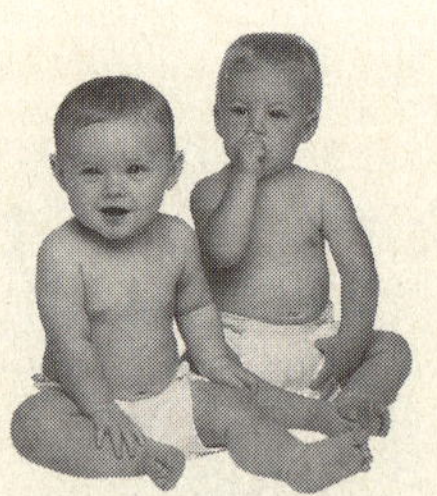

chief

cries

piece

flies

babies

Read this sentence about the story. Circle the word that has the **long e** sound that you hear in **babies**. Draw a line under the word that has the **long i** sound that you hear in **tie**.

The movie tried to fool you.

Vocabulary — Synonyms and Antonyms

Words that mean almost the same thing are called **synonyms**. Read these sentences.

> They made everything around the kids very big. They built giant tables and chairs.

The words **giant** and **big** are synonyms.

Words that have opposite meanings are **antonyms**. Read this sentence from the story.

> When real kids stood next to these huge things, the kids looked tiny.

The words **huge** and **tiny** are antonyms.

© Buena Vista Pictures

Read these sentences. Look at the words in dark print. If they are opposites, write **A** for antonym. If they mean the same thing, write **S** for synonym.

_______ **1.** You may think it's **easy** to make kids look big in the movies. It's really very **hard**.

_______ **2.** People **like** to go to the movies. They **enjoy** movies very much.

_______ **3.** Making big and small movie magic is hard **work**. Some people think it's just **play**.

Words That Were New to You

Choose words from the story that were new to you. Use a dictionary to check the meanings. Add the words and their meanings to your word list on page 128.

REREADING

Sequence

Sometimes writers need to tell how something is done. When you read, ask yourself "What happened first?" "Then what happened?" "What happened last?" That will help you to follow the order.

You can make a chart to help you. Look at this chart. It shows how the movie makers made the kids look small enough to swim in a tiny puddle.

First	The movie makers got 13,000 pounds of dirt.
Then	They mixed the dirt with water to make 25,000 gallons of mud.
Last	They filmed the kids crossing the giant puddle.

Reread the story. Be sure you understand the order in which things happened. Then complete this chart to show how the movie makers made a baby look larger than a nine-story building.

First	
Then	
Last	

Word Referents

A **noun** names a person, place, or thing. A **pronoun** is a word that can stand for a noun. Read these sentences. Look at the pronoun in dark print. Circle the noun that the pronoun stands for.

1. A man makes a big mistake. **He** shrinks three kids.

2. In the movie, the baby walks down a city street. **He** looks much bigger than the buildings.

3. People in movies can look very tall. **They** can also look very small.

THINK and WRITE

Use what you have learned to complete one of these activities.

1. Have you seen a movie where someone gets very big or very small? Write what you thought of the movie. Tell why your friends should or should not see it.

2. Make up an ad for *Honey, I Shrunk the Kids*. In your ad, tell why people should see the movie.

3. What else would you like to know about movie magic? Think of some questions. Send them to the people who made *Honey, I Shrunk the Kids*. The address is
   The Walt Disney Studio Archives
   500 South Buena Vista Street
   Burbank, California 91521-1200

GETTING READY TO READ

You are about to read "Ben's Wish." Is there something very special that you wish for? Are you really sure you want your wish to come true?

What Do You Think You Will Learn?

Look at the pictures on pages 117 through 120. What do you think "Ben's Wish" will be about? What do you think that Ben wishes for? Write your ideas below.

____

____

____

____

____

Ben was taller than all the other kids in his school. He was even taller than his father!

"Hey, Big Ben," the kids would call. "How's the air up there?"

Ben wished he had a glass of water so he could pour it on them. Then he could say, "The air's fine, but it's raining!"

Ben wished that he could be the size of the other kids.

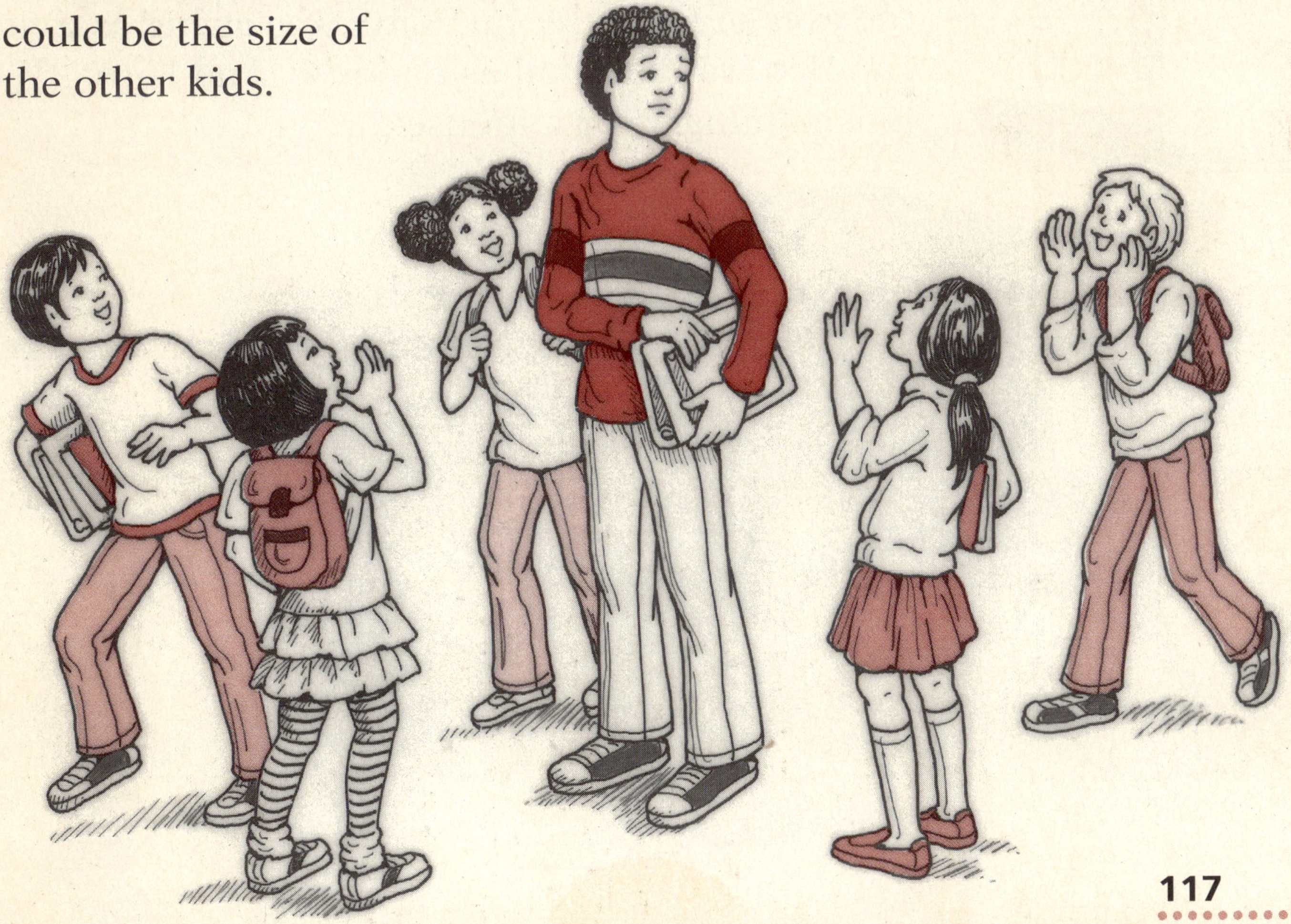

"If I were a little taller than the other kids, that would be okay," Ben thought. "But this is no fun! I'm too big to fit into the chairs in my classroom!"

His class was reading a book called *Alice in Wonderland*. In it, Alice has a drink that makes her smaller. Ben wished he had one, too.

Ben was still wishing when he walked home after school. He was still wishing when he had his after-school milk and cookies.

"I wish this milk was magic," Ben thought. "One gulp and I'd be smaller!"

Ben shut his eyes. He wished the milk was magic. Then he drank it in one big gulp.

Ben opened his eyes. He looked right into the eyes of Kitty the cat. Kitty was as big as a car. Ben was as small as a mouse. And Kitty looked hungry for a mouse.

Ben scooted under the refrigerator where the cat couldn't get him.

"Wow!" Ben said. "This is what people mean when they say be careful what you wish for."

Just then, the floor began to shake. Ben peeked out from under the refrigerator. He saw shoes as big as boats. And wearing the shoes was his little sister Lucy.

"Hello, Kitty," Lucy said. "Why are you sitting by the refrigerator? Are you hungry?"

"Sure," thought Ben. "Kitty wants a Benburger!"

Lucy filled a bowl with milk. She put it on the floor. Kitty drank some. Then she followed Lucy out of the kitchen.

Ben came out from his hiding place. He looked around. Everything was so BIG!

Bits of cookie on the floor looked like big rocks. Kitty's bowl of milk looked like a swimming pool. It gave Ben an idea.

"I'll jump into the milk pool," he said. "The milk might still be magic for me!"

Ben rolled some cookie rocks over to the milk bowl. He piled them up. Then he climbed to the top.

Ben looked down at the milk. He shut his eyes and wished real hard. Then he jumped!

SPLASH! CRASH! Ben was tall again! But the milk was spilled all over the floor. And Kitty's milk bowl was broken to bits.

"What was that noise?" Lucy asked as she ran into the room. "Oh! You broke the bowl!"

"I guess I'm too big for a milk bath," Ben said, smiling to himself.

AFTER READING

What Did You Learn?

You have read "Ben's Wish" for the first time. Now look back at what you wrote on page 116. Was Ben's wish what you thought it would be? What clues helped you make your guess? Were you surprised? What surprised you the most? Write your answers on the lines below.

____

____

____

Check Your Understanding

Read each sentence. Look at the words in the box. Choose one word to complete each sentence. Write the word on the correct line.

smaller	cat	Lucy	taller

1. Ben was _____________________ than all the other kids in his school.

2. Ben wished he could be _____________________.

3. Ben had to hide from his _____________________.

4. Ben told his sister _____________________ that he was too big to take a milk bath.

Word Analysis — Vowel Digraphs o͞o and o͝o

In some words the vowels **oo** have the sound that you hear in the word **book**.

In some words the vowels **oo** have the sound that you hear in the word **moon**.

Say each picture name. Listen for the vowel sound. Circle the words that have the same **oo** vowel sound that you hear in the word **moon**.

1. food	2. hook	3. tools	4. wood
5. stool	6. boot	7. broom	8. spoon

Read this sentence. Underline the word that has the **oo** sound that you hear in **book**. Circle the word that has the **oo** sound that you hear in **moon**.

He was still wishing when he had his

after-school milk and cookies.

Vocabulary — Contractions

Sometimes two words are put together to make a shorter word. The shorter word is called a **contraction**. An **apostrophe** takes the place of the missing letters in a contraction. An apostrophe looks like this '. Look at the words in the box.

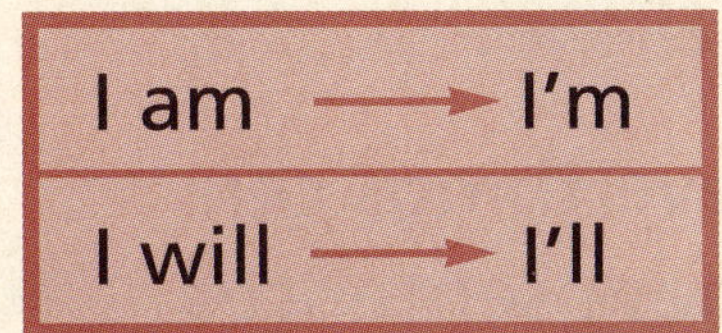

The word I'm is a contraction that stands for I am. The apostrophe stands for the letter a in am. The word I'll is a contraction that stands for I will. The apostrophe stands for the letters wi in the word will.

Read these sentences. Darken the circle next to the words that stand for the contraction in dark print.

1. Ben **didn't** want to be so tall.

   Ⓐ did not   Ⓑ can not   Ⓒ could not

2. "One gulp and **I'd** be smaller!" Ben thought.

   Ⓐ I am   Ⓑ I will   Ⓒ I would

3. The cat **couldn't** get Ben.

   Ⓐ can not   Ⓑ could not   Ⓒ would not

Words That Were New to You

Choose words from the story that were new to you. Use a dictionary to check the meanings. Add the words and their meanings to your word list on page 128.

REREADING

Reality and Fantasy

Some stories are about things that could happen in real life. These stories are **real**. Other stories are about things that could not happen in real life. These stories are **make-believe**.

Sometimes real and make-believe things can happen in the same story. Read these sentences about "Ben's Wish."

1. Ben was taller than his father.

2. Ben was as small as a mouse.

Which sentence is about something that could really happen? Which sentence is about something that could not really happen? Ben could be taller than his father. But Ben could not be as small as a mouse. So, sentence 1 is real and sentence 2 is make-believe.

Read the story again. Ask yourself what is real and what is make-believe. Then read the sentences below. On the line before each sentence, write **R** if it is real. Write **M** if it is make-believe.

_______**1.** Ben was too tall to fit into the chairs in his classroom.

_______**2.** Ben drank a magic drink that made him get very small.

_______**3.** Ben jumped into a bowl of milk to get tall again.

Dialogue

The words that people say in a story are called **dialogue**. Read the sentences below. Find the sentences in the story. Find the name of the person who said these words. Write the name on the line.

1. "This is what people mean when they say be careful what you wish for." (page 119) _______________________

2. "Hello, Kitty." (page 119) _______________________

3. "What was that noise?" (page 120) _______________________

4. "I guess I'm too big for a milk bath." (page 120)

____

THINK and WRITE

Use what you have learned to complete one of these activities.

1. Think of something you have wished for. What do you think would happen if your wish came true? Write about your ideas.

2. Suppose you suddenly became very, very small. Tell how your classroom would look to you.

3. Would you rather be very, very tall or very, very small? Tell why.

MY WORD LIST

MY WORD LIST

MY WORD LIST